ONE SMALL STEP

"You want a leg up?"

"Of course not."

One, two, three bounces on her right foot, her right hand on the cantle, and Sharon hefted herself up. Halfway there, her left foot gave out, slipping out of the stirrup. She slid back to the ground, landing heavily on both legs. Lightning bolts of pain shot up her bones. But wincing was out of the question. Instead Sharon gave the crowd a gritted-teeth grin.

She heard people whispering, that concerned *tut-tut* noise she hated. Sharon looked over at her tentmates. Melissa was chewing on her lower lip. Jenna was giving her an atta-girl grin. When Katie saw Sharon looking her way, she gave her a small, barely perceptible nod of encouragement.

Sharon repositioned herself. The whispering picked up, like a rush of wind through a dry field.

"For those of you taking bets," Sharon said loudly, "the current odds are five to two I fall flat on my face."

The whispering stopped. Sharon eased her foot back into the stirrup and, with a grunt of effort, hoisted herself up and over in one fluid movement.

A few people gasped. Some smiled. Some still looked doubtful. Sharon glanced over at Katie. Katie nodded again. She, for one, didn't look at all surprised.

SILVER CREEK RIDERS

Back in the Saddle

Beth Kincaid

JOVE BOOKS, NEW YORK

SILVER CREEK RIDERS: BACK IN THE SADDLE

A Jove Book / published by arrangement with
the author

PRINTING HISTORY
Jove edition / September 1994

All rights reserved.
Copyright © 1994 by Jove Publications, Inc.
Cover illustration by Patti Cosgrove.
This book may not be reproduced in whole
or in part, by mimeograph or any other means,
without permission. For information address:
The Berkley Publishing Group, 200 Madison Avenue,
New York, New York 10016.

ISBN: 0-515-11480-4

Jove Books are published by The Berkley Publishing Group,
200 Madison Avenue, New York, New York 10016.
JOVE and the "J" design are trademarks
belonging to Jove Publications, Inc.

PRINTED IN THE UNITED STATES OF AMERICA

10 9 8 7 6 5 4 3 2 1

Back in the Saddle

Prologue

Tires screeched. A bottle shattered. Drunken laughter filled the still dusk air. Even before she spun around in her saddle, Sharon knew she was in trouble.

A mile back a sky-blue Ford truck careened wildly from side to side on the narrow country road. Another bottle, tossed from an open window, burst into green splinters. Someone hooted.

Sharon eased Cassidy to a stop on the thin strip of grass lining the road. "Hang in there, baby," she whispered, stroking Cass's neck, still hot from their gallop through the field a half mile back.

Cassidy shifted and strained, her whole body on alert. She hated cars, always had. They both dreaded this one-mile stretch of road, but it was the only route back from a heavenly meadow full of sweet red clover.

The truck strayed into the other lane, bearing down on a little red Toyota. Sharon gasped, squeezing her reins. A horn blared. Tires squealed. The truck lurched back just an instant short of disaster.

"We're fine here, Cass," Sharon said, but her voice was just a shadow of itself. Still, Cass was waiting

1

patiently, hard as it was for her, waiting for Sharon to signal what to do.

The truck was two hundred yards and closing fast. Frantically, Sharon searched to her right for safe haven. Nothing, just a steep ditch, washed deep from fall rains. And on the other side of the ditch, a barbed-wire fence tangled with thick mats of sharp-needled bushes.

"Horse meat!" someone yelled. Sharon turned. In the shadowy light she could just make out the driver's eyes. Crazy, drunk probably, and filled with something dark that sent a cold spasm through her heart.

She knew, somehow she knew, he was going to try to run them off the road.

Sharon nudged Cass toward the ditch, carefully, slowly, as slowly as she dared. Cassidy hesitated. It was nearly dark, and the pit was deep.

"That's my baby," Sharon urged, and they started down tentatively. "It's going to be okay."

This is good, Sharon thought, *we'll be fine, after all,* and then the bottle crashed just inches from Cassidy's rear legs.

Cass reared up and back and the world was nothing but the sound of scraping metal and shrill brakes and shattering glass and, most horrifying of all, a sound like dry twigs cracking, the sound of breaking bones.

An unreal silence followed. Sharon lay still, waiting. She felt something heavy on her chest, and as night closed in on her, cold and black, she realized it was Cassidy's head she felt on top of her, still hot, still smelling of clover and sweat and leather, but no longer moving at all.

1

Melissa Hall strolled past each stall in the big old stable, inhaling the sweet scent of worn leather and warm hay as if it were an exotic perfume. Silver Creek lacked the class of Sycamore Farms, her old stable back in Maryland. No engraved brass name tags on each stall door, no skylights, no climate-controlled tack room. But one thing was the same—that wonderful, intoxicating smell.

Entering this old barn was like stepping off a merry-go-round onto solid ground. Here, everything made sense. Out there, out in the world of parents and school and friends and enemies, nothing did. Here, all that mattered was you and your horse and how you moved together. Out there, other things mattered. Things like the color of your skin.

Melissa sauntered down the aisle, greeting each horse, reading the little carved wooden plaques on the stall doors and committing the names to memory. Say-So, a gentle bay gelding, seemed especially eager to get acquainted. Jenkins, the gray mare next door, eyed Melissa doubtfully, prancing back and forth

3

skittishly in her stall. Melissa took her time with Jenkins, holding out her hand to let the mare get to know her scent, sweet-talking her until Jenkins relented and allowed Melissa to stroke her delicate muzzle.

A good lineup, Melissa decided. Quality, well-cared-for horses. Not the expensive stock they'd had at Sycamore Farms, horses with pedigrees a mile long. But nice enough.

The morning sun poured through the arched window over the stable door, a butter-colored tube of light that looked solid enough to lean on. Melissa shaded her eyes. The horse in the last stall caught her attention. In the fall palette of the stable—duns and creams and chestnuts and roans—the piebald mare stood out. Her black coat was splotched with white, as if someone had tossed pints of paint on her hide.

"Foxy," Melissa read. The mare sauntered over, looked Melissa up and down, considered. Melissa held out her hand. Foxy snorted, then did a little soft-shoe across her stall.

"Gotta watch that one," came a raspy woman's voice.

An older woman, maybe sixty, came down the aisle. She was short and stocky but moved with a confident grace. She wore a Mets baseball cap and a T-shirt that said *Have you hugged your horse today?*

"I'm sorry," Melissa said. "I guess maybe I'm not supposed to be here. I know the camp brochure said noon, but I got here early—" Her voice trailed off. "I sort of have this thing about being early."

"Nothing wrong with that." The woman stopped at a nearby stall to examine the ear of a black mare.

"Lost time is never found again."

Melissa nodded politely, even though she had no idea what that meant.

"Rose Donovan." Finished with her exam of the mare, the woman extended her hand. Her palm was warm and callused. Melissa wondered if she was a stablehand. More likely a retired stablehand. "What do you think of the place?"

"Well, I haven't seen much, but I like it so far."

"Good answer. I own it."

Melissa smiled nervously. "I, uh, forgot to introduce myself. I'm Melissa Hall."

"I know. I make it a point to know who all my riders are. Especially the good ones." Rose looked her up and down. "The New England Classic. Reserve champion."

Melissa thought back to the camp application form. *Tell us a little bit about your riding background . . . Please include a photo with your application . . . Why do you want to spend your summer at Silver Creek?*

I don't, Melissa had written. Her mother had made her cross it out.

"The Classic is quite a competition," Rose continued. "You should be mighty proud."

Melissa shook her head. "Actually, I blew it in the jump-off."

"Second to a legend like Sharon Finnerty," Rose said. "No shame in that." She pointed to Foxy. "You've got good taste. Foxy's the smartest horse in the stable."

"She's got an attitude, all right."

"Former polo pony," Rose said, rolling her eyes. "She expects her feed in a sterling silver bucket."

Silence fell. Melissa wondered if she should leave. Maybe Rose was just being polite, not telling her to beat it. "Well," she said. "I should go unpack, I suppose."

Rose was still staring at Foxy. "Foxy here's the only piebald we've got at the moment."

Melissa smiled ruefully. "I know how she feels."

"We're lucky to have her here," Rose said. "Makes this old place a little more interesting." With a tilt of her cap, she headed off.

Melissa sighed. She said good-bye to Foxy and followed Rose out into the bright sunlight. Several cars had pulled into the curved gravel driveway that circled in front of the stable. Campers piled out, laughing, stretching their legs, tossing their bedrolls and suitcases onto the drive. Different ages, different shapes and sizes, and, no doubt, different riding skills.

But there was one thing they all had in common. They were all white.

Melissa turned away, following the cool, tree-shaded path to her tent. This wasn't the first time she'd felt out of place since moving to rural New York. And it probably wouldn't be the last.

Her mom called it the if-only game. If only Melissa's parents hadn't divorced, then her mom wouldn't have decided to uproot Melissa and move her back to this godforsaken backwater where Ms. Hall had vacationed as a kid. If only they hadn't been so distracted by all the divorce stuff, Melissa wouldn't have missed her deadline for Saxony Riding Camp, the one she usually attended, the one everyone wanted to get into, and she wouldn't be stuck here at Silver Creek with a bunch of strangers who probably didn't know which end of a horse was which without a map.

She reached the broad meadow that bordered Silver Lake. Big army tents were scattered here and there, billowing in the breeze like ugly green sailboats in a sea of grass.

She stepped into her hot, airless tent. At Saxony she'd roomed in a beautiful converted Victorian farmhouse. She'd had an antique bed with feather pillows and a private bath with a clawfoot bathtub.

Here at Silver Creek, she had a tent that smelled like an overripe gym sock. As for the bathrooms, she had yet to locate any. She wondered if they were supposed to bathe in the lake.

Enough with the whining, Mel, she told herself firmly. She was going to make this work. She didn't have a choice. If she was disciplined, if she worked hard enough, she could make everything come out okay. It was the same way she won ribbons. It was the same way she got straight A's.

If you put your mind to it, you can do anything. Her mom had always told her that when Melissa was growing up. Not necessarily a good thing to tell a very literal six-year-old. Melissa had put her mind to the idea that she could fly, and had broken three fingers and an ankle soaring off the garage into a Hefty bag full of garbage. Eventually, of course, she'd figured out a better way to fly—sailing over a fence on the back of an airborne horse.

She'd found a way to fly. She'd make this work, too.

Melissa surveyed the dusty, cramped tent. Four cots, four battered bureaus. When in doubt, organize. She opened her neatly packed suitcase and pulled out her camera, her laptop computer, her box of stationery, and the book of poems by Maya Angelou that her mother had given her. Last, but most definitely not least, came her two brass-framed photos. Aisha and Chelsea, her two best friends, with Melissa at the New England Classic. And Melissa with Marcus, her boyfriend for the last year and a half, at her going-away party.

Loneliness washed over her like an icy wave. She missed them so. She missed everything about her old life.

"This is your new life," she muttered. "So get on with it, already."

She continued unpacking, placing neat piles of clothes into her bureau. At the bottom of her suitcase, she discovered several boxes of Cracker Jack. She loved popcorn in any form and scarfed it down by the ton.

There was a Post-it note on the top box. *Just try your best,* it read. *That's all I ever ask. Have loads of fun. Love you, Mom.*

Of course, sometimes her best wasn't quite good enough. She gazed at the photo taken at the Classic. She was holding her ribbon high, its red, yellow, white, and pink streamers nearly hiding her face as she grinned for the camera. But even now she remembered her anger at herself as she'd watched Sharon Finnerty walk away with the championship.

What kind of riders would her three tentmates turn out to be? Melissa wondered. Suddenly she had an idea. She grabbed three boxes of Cracker Jack and placed one on each cot. Sort of a welcome-to-the-overripe-gym-sock present to her new roomies.

Melissa returned to her cot and lay back, admiring

her handiwork. Who knew? Maybe it would help break the ice.

And maybe someday I'll really fly, she added grimly.

He was waiting for her, just like she knew he would be.

Jenna McCloud dropped her bike at the entrance to Hilltop Farm and ran up the steep gravel hill to the lower paddock. Turbo greeted her with a soft whinny and a determined nudge of his soft red-gold muzzle.

"All right, already," Jenna said, digging through her worn denim backpack. "I've got your carrot in here somewhere. You sure you're not part pig?"

Turbo lifted his head disdainfully.

"Hey, lighten up. Just a little human humor."

At last she located Turbo's carrot. A well-chewed piece of Juicy Fruit was stuck to the end of it. Jenna peeled it off and fed the carrot to Turbo, sighing as he munched contentedly.

She scratched the five-pointed white star on his forehead. He was beautiful. From the beginning, she'd been right about that. Nice conformation, clean, graceful lines. When she'd seen the FOR SALE sign on the bulletin board in the Silver Creek tack room, she'd nearly drooled. Even in the photo you could tell he was a classy guy.

Now it was her turn to take a picture. She retrieved her Polaroid camera from her backpack, annoyed by the tear that spilled down her cheek when she bent down. She'd promised herself she was not going to pull some wimped-out, whiny bawling number. At least, not in front of Turbo.

"Come on, guy, show me a little beefcake," she urged, clearing her throat. "Sorry, wrong species again."

Turbo eyed her suspiciously. She depressed the button and the camera whirred. Moments later it spat out a shiny, ghostly blur. She watched impatiently, waiting for the image to surface like a fish rising slowly from the bottom of a murky pond.

He was supposed to be hers. She'd been arranging it for months like a high-finance deal. Her parents had agreed to put up half. Jenna was going to add all her savings, three years' worth of helping out at her mother's restaurant. She'd promised to give up birthday and Christmas presents for the next two years. And she was going to work an extra Saturday afternoon a month bussing tables, saving her parents even more money. To top it all off, there was her bequest from Great-aunt Milly on her father's side, who'd had the gracious timing to die at the ripe old age of ninety-eight and leave Jenna all her worldly savings just as Turbo had gone up for sale.

It was complicated, it was conniving, it was brilliant. Jenna had lobbied and pleaded and brokered deals. She had convinced Mr. Shelby, Turbo's owner, to give her enough time to work out the details. And she had assured him that no one could ride Turbo like she could. A horse with that power, that cocky, rebellious attitude of his, needed someone like her to psych him out and let him be everything he could be.

And she had convinced Turbo to fall in love with her. Carrot by carrot, stroke by stroke. She had only ridden him a few times—something about Mr. Shelby's insurance—but that had been plenty. He was almost too much horse for her, and she loved him for it. (Of course, she'd assured her parents he was just a big overgrown My Little Pony, without the pastel tail.)

She swiped at another tear. The picture was slowly coming into focus. Turbo gazed back at her, ears pricked forward, his expression just slightly blurred, as if he weren't quite sure how he felt. She looked up at the real Turbo. The picture didn't do him justice, not even close.

She climbed onto the white fence and Turbo leaned over her shoulder. "See this?" She held up the photo. Turbo smelled it, considered it as an hors d'oeuvre, then settled for a nuzzle of Jenna's short brown hair. "You could be a male model, Turb. On the cover of *Horse Beautiful.*"

She scratched his chin and sniffled. Up the road, she could see Mr. Shelby on his front porch. He waved hesitantly. He probably knew she was here to say good-bye.

"Look, Turb, there's something we need to discuss," Jenna said. "I know we had big plans, guy. Lots of fun, some laughs, maybe the Triple Crown. But"—she cleared her throat again and Turbo flicked his ears—"well, there's been a slight change of plans. Business is bad, and my parents can't spare the money right now because my little sister goes to this special school year-round and the tuition just went up, and see, Mr. Shelby needs to sell you right away because *he* needs the money, and oh, man, am I babbling or what?"

She stared into his huge melted-chocolate eyes. Turbo looked away, glaring at a fat orange cat with the nerve to saunter through his territory. There was no way she could make him understand. But then,

Jenna wasn't sure she understood, either.

Nobody said life was fair, her dad had told her. There will be other horses. When life hands you lemons, make lemonade. When he'd gotten to that tired cliché, she'd zoned out. Her father just didn't get it. There would never be another Turbo.

Jenna began to cry, in spite of her best intentions. She buried her face in his strong, silky neck and sobbed till Turbo's coat was wet with her tears.

She heard the crunch of gravel and yanked away. No way could she let Mr. Shelby see her like this.

"Figured you'd be here."

Katie. Thank goodness. She didn't mind if Katie saw her cry. They'd been friends since first grade. In six years they'd bawled together plenty of times.

"You got a Kleenex?" Jenna asked.

Katie shook her head, brushing a long tendril of black curly hair behind her ear. She reached into her jeans pocket. "Would you settle for a granola bar wrapper?"

"I'll stick with my sleeve."

"Hi, Turb," Katie said softly. She leaned against the fence. Turbo stretched out his neck between them, reveling in a joint ear scratch.

"It's not fair," Jenna muttered.

Katie nodded. "I know." She smiled her wide, sweet, understanding smile.

"Life sucks."

"Well, I don't know if I'd go that far—"

"Don't start with me, Katie. I already had the when-life-gives-you-lemons speech this morning while I was packing for camp. But this is not about citrus fruit. It's about a horse. This horse. My horse."

Katie kicked at the ground. She was lanky and tall, much taller than Jenna. "Maybe we could hide him in your bedroom. We could muck out your closet now and then and he could sleep in your bed with you. Who'd notice?"

"I'd have a heck of a time hosing him down in my bathtub." Jenna sighed and looked away. Above them in a tree, a mourning dove cooed. "Listen, Katie. I've been thinking. I may blow off horse camp."

"We're supposed to leave in two hours!" Katie cried. "Don't toy with me, Jen. You know I'm emotionally vulnerable right now."

"You? *I'm* the one who just lost the next Derby winner."

"Well, *I'm* the one who can barely keep her seat at a walk, and there's no way I'm going to camp without you there for moral support."

"You've been taking lessons at Silver Creek for months," Jenna argued. "You know all the horses. You know the instructors. What are you worried about?"

"Everything. I'm worried about everything. What if I end up in a tent with a bunch of horse snobs who've ridden for years and they short-sheet my cot—"

"Come on. You can do better than that. What if they're all Olympic gold medalists? What if they threaten you with their riding crops and force you to shine their boots every morning?"

"That's why I need you along. To beat them up." Katie combed Turbo's mane with her fingers. "We've been dreaming about this all spring, Jenna. We're talking twenty-four hours a day with horses for practically an entire summer."

"But not with *this* horse."

"Riding, every single day, Jenna. Swimming. Riding. Hiking. Riding."

"Ticks the size of lab rats."

"Trail riding, grooming our own horses, cavaletti work—"

Jenna grimaced. "Mosquitoes the size of 747s."

"Archery. Riding. Arts and crafts. Riding. Did I mention riding?"

Jenna stroked Turbo's neck, staring off into space. "Do you think they'll force us to make lanyards? Because I will not, under any circumstances, make a lanyard."

"What's a lanyard?"

"It's one of those crafty things you send to your parents so they know they're getting their money's worth."

Katie grabbed Jenna's knees. "So you're going? You promise?"

"Yeah, I'm going. But I have absolutely no intention of enjoying it."

"That's OK. I'll enjoy it enough for both of us." Katie frowned. "I hope." She looked at her watch. "I gotta go. Rae wants to help me finish packing. She thinks I need guidance."

Jenna rolled her eyes. Katie's stepmother was big on guidance. "What are you packing, anyway?"

"My trunk."

"Your trunk? It's not like we're going to the Himalayas, Katie."

"Rae's making me bring all this reading material. I'm supposed to read a book a week. It's part of the deal, remember? I skip the tutor thing and go to horse camp, Rae and my dad get weekly book reports."

"This is all I'm packing," Jenna said, taking the picture of Turbo from her jeans pocket.

Katie looked at the picture, then up at Turbo's elegantly arched neck and regal stance. "He really is a beautiful horse, Jenna," she said softly. "I'm sorry it didn't work out."

Jenna reached around Turbo's neck and gave him a long, fierce hug. "Bye, Turb," she whispered.

She jumped down, grabbed her camera and her backpack, and headed down the gravel path with Katie by her side. By the time they reached their bikes, both girls were crying freely, tears streaming down their faces like a sudden afternoon storm.

"Here," Katie said, sniffling. She handed Jenna her granola bar wrapper.

Jenna tried to smile, but she couldn't. She climbed on her bike and didn't look back, not even for one last glimpse, not even when Turbo nickered for her softly as she sped away down the road.

2

"What'd you pack in this sucker? A spare horse?" asked Margaret Stone as she helped Katie lug her trunk down the path to the tent camp. Margaret, a petite woman with boyishly cut blond hair, was Katie's favorite riding instructor at Silver Creek.

"You know Be-Prepared-Katie," Jenna muttered. "I'll give you ten to one she's got a first-aid kit and a fire extinguisher in there."

"Please," Katie said. "Give me some credit, will you?" She grinned at Margaret. "The fire extinguisher's in my backpack."

They came to a clearing. Katie and Margaret paused to catch their breath. "It's beautiful," Katie murmured.

"It's not like you haven't seen Silver Lake a thousand times," Jenna said, marching past.

"What's with her?" Margaret whispered.

"Turbo." Katie mouthed his name. She watched her friend barrel ahead. Jenna was small and muscular, always moving and talking at light speed, but today she strode along like her body was made of coiled springs.

Katie gazed at the big curved lake that shone like a blue half-moon. Beyond it towered Lookout Mountain, so thick with dark green pines it was nearly black.

Huddled on the edge of the lake sat the big olive-colored tents where the girls would be staying. They were bigger than Katie had imagined, with large flaps opened to the breeze.

"I pictured little pup tents," she said as they caught up with Jenna.

"All the comforts of home," Margaret said, "except for that new-fangled indoor plumbing."

"Easy for you to say," Jenna grumbled. "You get to sleep in the lodge."

"All the counselors do. Old age has it prerogatives. Besides, it's just a quick quarter-mile jaunt back to the bathrooms. It'll toughen you up."

"Where are the boys' tents?" Katie asked.

"Over there, across the creek on the other side," Margaret said. "And yes, that was deliberate."

"Don't get yourself all worked up, Katie," Jenna warned. "They're just like the guys at school. Same zits, same obscene jokes, only with riding boots." She looked at Margaret. "Katie's an incurable romantic."

"She'd better be. The ratio of girls to guys is three to one." Margaret pointed to the tent closest to the lake. "Over there is your new home away from home. Thoroughbred Tent. They're all named after a horse breed. Your next-door neighbors are Morgan Tent over there, and Arabian Tent next to the big pine."

"This is so weird," Katie said. "I've been coming to Silver Creek for lessons, for, I don't know, practically the whole school year. But *living* here for the whole summer, it's going to feel so different. When do we start riding?"

"Tomorrow morning," Margaret said. "Tryouts this afternoon."

"Tryouts?" Katie demanded. "Nobody said anything about tryouts!"

Margaret smiled understandingly. "Relax, Katie. It's just to help determine where to place all the campers. Not everyone here is a student from the area, remember. We have kids coming from all over the East Coast."

Katie's stomach twisted into a knot she knew she'd never get untied. "I hate tests," she murmured as they set down her trunk near the open front flap of the tent.

Jenna put her hand on her shoulder. "I know what you're doing, Katie. Panicking early to avoid the rush."

"But—"

"Don't sweat it. You're a solid rider, you know that. You've come a long way in just a few months."

"What if they separate us?"

"They won't."

"Knock, knock!" Margaret called.

Katie and Jenna peered inside. The tent was hot and shadowy. In the corner, a pretty African-American girl was dozing.

Jenna sauntered inside. "Very swanky," she said, dropping her backpack on the nearest cot. "But—" she curled her lip, "what exactly is this crud all over my pillow?"

The girl in the corner leapt up, suddenly alert. Her almond eyes went wide. "Oh," she said. "I must have dozed off. I'm Melissa. I guess you found the Cracker Jack."

"We found something, all right," Jenna said, tossing her pillow to the floor.

"My mom sent some extras in my suitcase and I figured it would be sort of a welcome-to-the-tent present."

"How sweet," Katie said.

"Nice of you to predigest it," Jenna added.

Melissa gazed around the room. "Wait a minute. Where are the boxes?"

Something let out a low, guttural burp. "Don't look at me," Margaret said. "I skipped the goulash surprise today."

Melissa sniffed the air. "Does it smell, um . . . a little *weird* in here? I mean, when I first got here, it sort of reminded me of those socks you find in the bottom of your gym locker at the end of the school year, you know? But this . . . this transcends mere gym sock."

"Don't look at me," Jenna said defensively. "I took a shower this morning." She frowned. "At least I think I did. I had a lot on my mind."

Katie pointed underneath the cot across from Melissa's. Four hooves protruded from under the blanket-draped bed. "Mischief," she said.

"Who?" Melissa asked.

"Silver Creek's resident garbage disposal. He's our goat mascot."

Jenna headed over for a closer look, but suddenly she went into a skid and lost her footing. Both feet flew in the air and she landed with a thud at the foot of Melissa's cot.

Melissa reached for her camera and snapped two shots for posterity.

"Walk much?" Margaret asked.

Jenna scowled at the bottom of her boot. "I walk plenty," she said. "But not in goat turd." She sighed. "Can I please go home now? And by the way, I want those pictures destroyed."

"Sorry," Melissa said. "It's a new camera and I can't seem to stop myself."

"Don't mind her," Katie told Melissa. "She's having a bad day."

"This is an omen," Jenna said. "I'm not meant to be here, Margaret. I should be at home on the couch watching Beavis and Butthead and drowning my sorrows in Chunky Monkey ice cream."

Margaret backed toward the tent flap. "I think this would be a fine time for me to discreetly leave," she said. "Nothing personal, but this place smells like a livestock show. But before I go, I'll take care of the introductions. I'm Margaret, teacher, occasional bookkeeper, and all-around great person." She draped an arm around Katie. "This is Katie Anderson, another all-around great person. The one with the alluring scent is Jenna McCloud." She reached into her back pocket. "And you must be—" She fumbled with a piece of paper.

"Melissa Hall," the girl in the corner finished for her.

"Don't tell me, I've almost got it," Margaret insisted.

"Really. I'm Melissa Hall."

Margaret scanned her list. "Wait a minute. Here it is! You're . . . Melissa Hall!"

Katie got down on her knees and reached under the cot to scratch Mischief's very full stomach. "Margaret's much better on horseback than she is with paperwork," she confided to Melissa.

"Now that I'm on a roll, your other tentmate's name is;—" Margaret consulted her list. "Sharon Something. Something fishy. Here it is. Finnerty. That's it."

"Sharon?" Melissa asked in surprise.

"You know her?" Jenna asked as she yanked off her boot.

"She's incredible," Melissa said. "I came in second to her at the New England Classic two years ago. She's got this beautiful bay mare, an absolutely amazing jumper." She looked over at Margaret. "I wonder if Sharon's bringing her?"

"We've got the room. Some riders do bring their own horses," Margaret said.

"That is, if they *have* their own horses," Jenna added darkly.

Mischief let out another half moan, half burp. "Can it, you compost heap," Jenna said, scowling at the goat peeking his head out from under the blanket.

"I wonder if he ate the prizes?" Katie asked.

"Well, I'll leave this happy little family," Margaret said. "Orientation at the lodge at one, tryouts at the barn immediately afterward, dinner at six."

"Let me just get this clear before you go," Jenna said. "Do we have to make lanyards?"

"What on earth is a lanyard?" Margaret asked. Without waiting for an answer, she gave a wave and dashed off.

Katie sat on the cot across from Melissa's. "You actually did that well at the Classic?" she asked.

"Well, I've ridden for a long, long time," Melissa said. "Since I was four. And the thing is, I was light-years behind Sharon. I mean, it was like she and that horse had some psychic link. It took your breath away—"

Someone appeared in the doorway, a tall, willowy girl with wavy copper hair. She was older than they were, maybe fourteen, Katie guessed, and striking in a way that made you wish you could be her for an afternoon, just to see what it would be like to have guys throw themselves at your feet in a big, drooling heap.

She stepped into the tent. There was something odd about the way she moved, an awkward limp that caused her whole body to shift forward and then back, like a tree fighting the wind.

Then Katie saw them. On each of her jeaned legs, the girl wore heavy plastic and metal braces.

Katie glanced over at Melissa. She was shaking her head just slightly. Her mouth was a tight line.

The girl waited. Her eyes had a dare waiting in them.

At last Melissa spoke. "Sharon?" she asked softly.

3

"Yours truly."

Sharon stared at the three girls staring back at her. They all had the usual embarrassed, unfocused, get-me-out-of-here look. She crossed her arms and waited. She liked to see how long it took people to look away. It was sort of a test of hers. *One one thousand, two one thousand, three . . .* Three seconds before they were all staring at their hands so they could make it very clear they were not staring at her legs. Just three. Not encouraging. Most people managed to hit four.

One of them, a pretty, black girl on the corner cot, looked familiar. "Melissa. Melissa Hall, right?" Sharon asked.

Melissa nodded. "You remember me?"

"Sure." Sharon started to sit on the nearest cot, then reconsidered. She put down her duffel bag and stayed put. "The Classic, two years ago. You nearly had me till that jump-off. You were good." She shrugged. "Of course, I still kicked your butt."

Melissa laughed. A polite silence followed. Every-

25

one looked at their hands again. *One one thousand, two one thousand* . . .

Melissa cleared her throat. "This is Katie, um—"

"Anderson," said a pale, ponytailed girl with a sweet Girl Scout smile. She had that I'll-be-your-best-friend-out-of-pity look. "Welcome to our humble tent." She paused. "Do you need a hand with anything?"

Right on target. In the year and a half since her accident, Sharon had developed an instinct for these things.

"I'm Jenna McCloud," said the other girl, a short gymnast-looking type with a pixie cut. The perky, the-glass-is-half-full-not-half-empty type, Sharon guessed. "Watch out for the turds on the floor and the goat slobber on your pillow," Jenna added sullenly.

Well, Sharon thought, maybe not quite so perky.

"I left some Cracker Jack on the cots and this goat ate it," Melissa explained somberly, pointing to the now-visible Mischief.

Melissa, Sharon wasn't so sure about. She was probably from the buck-up-and-get-on-with-your-life school. But who knew? Maybe someone here at Silver Creek would surprise her. Not that anybody ever had yet.

She turned toward her cot and began unloading her duffel bag. A public service, sort of. With her back to them, they could whisper about her unselfconsciously.

She pulled out her jeans, her T-shirts, her pain medicine. *One one thousand, two one thousand* . . . She couldn't hear the whispering, but she could *feel* it.

"Um, Sharon?" Melissa spoke up. "I was wondering . . ." Her voice trailed off.

Sharon twisted around. Sometimes it was faster to turn from the waist than to reposition her legs. "Let me guess," she said. "You're thinking I've changed somehow since you last saw me, right?"

Melissa looked over at Katie, who was, of course, looking at her hands. "Well, yes, now that you mention it—"

"You're thinking, hmmm, what could have possibly happened to that Sharon girl?" Sharon liked the sarcasm in her own voice. "Well, I'll save you the embarrassment of having to ask."

"I didn't really—"

"Oh, I don't mind. You were bound to ask eventually. The truth is, it was just an accident, really." Sharon tossed her hair from side to side, slowly running her fingers through the thick auburn waves. "I've switched mousses. Hard to believe the before and after, isn't it?"

No one spoke. A black fly buzzed furiously in one corner of the tent.

Sharon checked their faces.

There, finally. She'd done it. They were all looking at her legs, staring at the braces with a mixture of horror and pity and embarrassment.

"Actually, Sharon," Melissa said softly. "I was going to ask you something else."

Man, couldn't they leave it alone? "Yes?" Sharon snapped.

"I was wondering if you brought that beautiful bay of yours to camp. Cassidy, isn't that her name?"

Sharon reached into her duffel bag. She pulled out her journal. Then she found the videotape, the one her mom and dad and her physical therapist and her own good sense had told her not to bring along. The tape of Sharon and Cassidy at their last competition, soaring over jump after jump, dancing to some invisible music only they could hear.

"No," she answered at last, very quietly. "I didn't bring her."

A big mistake. That's what this was.

One by one, Sharon began to repack her belongings into her duffel bag. The others had left for orientation at the lodge. She'd insisted they go on ahead without her.

She would call her mom, tell her she'd changed her mind and to please come get her out of this second-rate camp with its second-rate riders. There would be a phone in the office. Everyone would be in the lodge doing the howdy-campers routine. They wouldn't even notice she'd left until it was too late.

She reached for a pair of socks, the thick wool ones she wore, even in the summer, to keep from chafing against her braces. Her mom would say she was chickening out. That Sharon was afraid she wouldn't be the rider she used to be. Which was not what this was about. She'd outgrown this juvenile camp stuff, that was all. She felt ten, a hundred, a thousand years older than Melissa and Jenna and Katie.

Besides, the last thing she needed was their pity.

If she wanted to ride, she could take private lessons. Well, okay, not right away. Money was tight, what with all her physical therapy. She could only afford to come to Silver Creek because they'd given her a partial scholarship. But eventually she'd find a way to ride, one way or another.

This camp thing had been Dr. Andropoulos's idea. Dr. A had dropped by during one of Sharon's physical therapy sessions and suggested, between leg lifts, that riding camp next summer would be just the thing for Sharon. The fresh air! The new friends! The strong leg muscles!

The endless pity. Dr. A had forgotten that one.

Sharon checked to make sure she hadn't left anything behind. She grabbed a last pair of socks and her journal. The journal had been Dr. A's idea, too. Dr. A was full of ideas. Write down your feelings, she'd said. Two days after the accident, no less. As if what Sharon really needed was a homework assignment.

But she'd done it. Mostly to keep everyone else at bay, everyone who kept telling her to share her pain with them. With her head buried in her journal, people left her alone. They assumed she was having Deep Thoughts.

She thumbed through the blue fabric-covered journal. Most of the pages were filled. She scanned the first entry. The ink was smeared. Tears? She didn't remember crying, not since those first few hours in intensive care. She certainly hadn't cried much in the long months after that.

Sharon looked away. As she was leaving, her mom had slipped the journal into Sharon's duffel bag to read, a reminder of how far Sharon had come in nineteen months. But she didn't need a walk down memory lane. She remembered just fine, thank you. Every last excruciating, horrifying moment.

She started to close the book, but a heading caught her eye. *Day 3*, it read, in her messy scrawl made even worse by all the painkillers.

The third day after That Day. She'd started numbering the days afterward, as if her life could be divided into neat sections—before That Day, and after That Day. It was never "the accident," or "when I was hurt," or "when Cassidy was killed." It was just That Day.

Sharon sat down on the edge of her cot. It had been months since she'd last written in this book. And she'd never actually read back a single word she'd written.

Reluctantly, Sharon began to read the first few lines. It was like watching a horror movie. You knew something awful was going to happen and you didn't want to see it, but somehow you couldn't keep your eyes off the screen.

Only this time, she was in the starring role.

Day 2
Oh, man, they just gave me more pills, those little ones that make me so doped up I can't remember my own name. They keep saying this'll stop the pain, but I don't care about the pain in my legs because that's real and it's mine and I can deal with that. It's the hurting I can't touch, it's Cassidy, it's all Cassidy.

Maybe I could bear it if I could just touch her one more time and say I love you and you're my whole world, maybe then I could let her go. If I could just say good-bye first. If I could just say you made me the rider I am, it was all you all along. I got all the ribbons and the dusty trophies crowding up my room, but it was really you. You made me so happy, Cass. You.

They didn't tell me she died right away. I was pretty out of it for a while. I kept saying, "Is she okay, is she okay," and they would ask me what year it was and I would say 1922. Or how old I was and I would say something like nine. So they thought I was too messed up to be told. But I knew anyway. I think I knew on the highway, before I passed out, when I felt her head on me. It was like when the sun goes behind a cloud and it's still day but there's something missing, somehow the light has changed and you miss it and you're waiting for it to come back.

Only it never will.

I'm so tired. I'm so so so so so tired. I want to go home I want to stop hurting I want Cass. I just want Cass.

The journal was heavy in her hands. Sharon put it down. Her leg twinged, as if words about pain could make it appear. But she didn't feel anything inside, not at all. It was like reading someone else's story.

All that emotion, all that grief. What had happened to it?

Somehow she'd packed it away, like she'd packed her duffel bag. It was the only way she could go back to being who she was. She'd stowed it away, and done her rehab, and gotten on with her life. And now, here she was at Silver Creek, as if nothing had ever happened.

Her leg throbbed, like a hot bulb switching on and off. She adjusted her left brace. Maybe her mom had been right about the journal. Reading it back, Sharon realized that she had come a long way. She was tough now. She had a wall around her like the hard casings protecting her legs.

Slowly, deliberately, Sharon unpacked her duffel bag another time. She'd stay for a while, but she'd do it on her terms. No help. And no pity. Nobody had any right to pity her. She was as good a rider as she'd ever been. And she was tougher than most people would ever be.

She'd handled That Day.

She could certainly handle today.

4

"Remember that old movie where the guy rents a hunting lodge for the winter?" Jenna asked. She paused outside the threshold of the lodge with Jenna and Melissa. "You know? The one where he goes crazy and hacks his family to bits with a chain saw?"

"Don't remind me," Katie said. She hated movies that starred sharp implements.

"Sorry. But that's what this place reminds me of," Jenna said. She stepped inside and Katie and Melissa followed.

It wasn't exactly the Holiday Inn, Katie had to admit, but she kind of liked the odd driftwood chandelier suspended from the rafters and the big stone fireplace, with the trophies and horse memorabilia lining the mantel. Long rows of wooden tables with benches filled most of the room. Overstuffed chairs, a Ping-Pong table, and a large TV sat next to the fireplace.

Already the room was filling up with campers. Margaret had been right—there were more girls than guys. The guys hugged the edges of the room in small groups. Katie noticed three friends from her weekly riding class and waved.

Melissa paused to snap a picture of the lodge. "You're not going to be doing that constantly, are you?" Jenna asked.

"Probably. I was on the school newspaper staff last year, and I sort of got into the habit." Melissa studied the room. "I guess you two know just about everyone here."

"Not really," Katie said, noting the uneasiness in Melissa's voice. "I mean, a lot of people are local, like us. They've been taking lessons at Silver Creek during the school year. But for riding camp in the summer, people come from all over. Rose is really well known for running a first-rate operation."

"I met her," Melissa said as the three girls sat down at an empty table near the fireplace. "At first I thought she was a stablehand."

Katie laughed. "She'd take that as a great compliment. She told me once she's happiest when she's just mucking out a stall—that is, next to when she's on a horse. She grumbles a lot, but I think she really loves this place."

Margaret walked past their table and paused, sniffing the air. "What's that I smell?" she asked Claire Donovan, another teacher. "Eau de goat?"

Jenna grimaced. "What's holding up the works, anyway? We're here to be oriented. So orient, already."

"Just hold your horses, McCloud," Claire said. "We're waiting on Mom."

"That's Rose's daughter, Claire," Katie explained as they walked away. "See that picture on the mantel over there? That's Claire with Wishful Thinking, her mount, at the last Olympic trials for the U.S. Equestrian Team. They made it to the finals. Claire's an amazing rider."

"A great teacher, too," Jenna added. "She teaches all the intermediate and advanced classes." She sniffed at her T-shirt. "Tell me the truth. Do I reek?"

Katie shrugged. "Not any more than usual."

Melissa nudged Katie and nodded toward the door. "There's Sharon." She waved, but Sharon ignored her. She walked slowly over to a table at the far end of the room and sat down.

"I asked her to walk over with us," Katie said. "I wish she wouldn't sit all by herself like that."

"What happened to her, anyway?" Jenna asked.

"I don't have a clue," Melissa said. "It's not like we were friends or anything—more like friendly competitors. I ran into her at a couple of the bigger New England shows. The last time I saw her was at the Classic."

"It must be so hard, getting around like that," Katie said. She lowered her voice. "Do you think she can still . . . well, ride?"

"She wouldn't be here if she couldn't, would she?" Jenna asked.

"The question is," Melissa said, "can she ride as well as she used to? To tell you the truth, I was kind of surprised when Margaret told us she was coming to this camp. I would have expected Sharon to be at one of the more elite camps, like Saxony." She sighed. "That's where I was supposed to go, except that . . . things got kind of mixed up."

"What do you mean, more *elite*?" Jenna demanded, her hazel eyes firing up like hot coals. "Silver Creek is one of the best riding camps in the country. I've been riding here for three and a half years, so trust me. In fact, it's *the* best, if you ask me—"

"Melissa didn't mean anything," Katie interrupted.

Jenna crossed her arms over her chest. "I'm just not in the mood for a bunch of sloppyseats who show up here bad-mouthing Silver Creek, with their horses they don't care for and ride once a month and don't even deserve—"

"I don't even have a horse!" Melissa cried. "And what exactly *is* a sloppyseat?"

"That's Jenna's name for the rich kids who own a horse just for the sake of owning a horse," Katie explained.

Melissa smiled knowingly. "I know the type. We had plenty of those at my old stable in Baltimore."

"I figured you weren't from Miller Falls," Jenna said, "or we would have seen you around."

"That's where Jenna and I live," Katie explained. "Just a few miles from here."

Melissa drew an invisible map on the table with her index finger. "Miller Falls is up here, right?"

"Yeah," Katie said. "Right next to that dried ketchup splotch."

"I live in Pooleville," Melissa said. "Right around here." She moved her finger an inch.

"More toward the knothole," Katie said. "But you're close."

Melissa sighed. "Sorry. We just moved here a few weeks ago. I'm still trying to get the lay of things. It's so easy in the city, but here, everywhere I look, it's nothing but trees."

"You got something against trees?" Jenna asked.

"No," Melissa said. "It just seems to me you could use a little more cement around here. I mean, what do you do for fun? Till the soil? Reap the crops?"

"We ride," Jenna said curtly. "Even if we aren't *elite* about it."

Melissa leaned back against the table, frowning. Jenna stared out the window, frowning. Katie stared at Jenna, glaring. She was annoyed at her best friend for picking fights all day. Melissa didn't deserve Jenna's temper, just because Jenna was upset about Turbo. Come to think of it, Katie didn't deserve her temper, either.

"It must be hard, moving to a whole new place like this," Katie said to Melissa.

Melissa managed a smile. "It's funny what you miss. I miss the Orioles. And I miss the loud noises you get in a city. The people and the traffic—"

"The sirens and the screams for mercy," Jenna interjected.

Melissa ignored her. She looked over at Sharon, who was still sitting by herself. "Sharon's from a small town, I think. Last I knew, she was living in Vermont. I wonder how she ended up here."

"I wonder why she didn't bring her horse along," Katie added.

"It's too bad," Melissa said. "She's an amazing horse." She turned to Jenna, who was drumming her fingers on the table while her legs bounced to a different beat. "Do either of you own a horse?"

"I don't," Katie spoke up quickly. "I've only been riding this last school year and I'm not exactly what you'd call a brilliant equestrian yet. I sort of have two left feet, and left hands, and left arms—"

Melissa laughed. "Don't worry. It gets easier."

"The thing is, I love horses. I mean, I *adore* them," Katie said. "All animals, actually. I have this mini-zoo at home. But owning a horse—well, I'm not quite ready for the responsibility."

"What about you, Jenna?" Melissa asked. Katie attempted a not-a-good-idea look, but it was too late.

Jenna stopped drumming her fingers. "I *had* a horse," she said. "And now I don't." She stood abruptly. "There's Kara over there. I'm going to go say hi."

Melissa watched her stalk away. "Are you two close?" she asked Katie.

"Best buds since first grade."

"Nothing personal, but what exactly do you see in her?"

"Jenna? Don't mind her. She's not usually this way. Well, I mean, she always loud and outspoken, but she's not usually such a—"

"Witch?" Melissa offered sweetly.

"See, right before camp, she was supposed to buy this great horse. She had it all worked out with her parents, everything was all set, and then all of a sudden they told her they couldn't afford it right now. She's got a little sister—she's adorable—named Allegra. She's retarded, and she goes to this special school year-round, but the tuition just went up. Jenna's parents own this health-food restaurant called McCloud Nine, and business is kind of bad right now. Even the extra her dad gets from teaching at the community college couldn't cover it. Anyway, Jenna's taking it pretty hard."

Melissa seemed to soften. "That's really too bad," she said. "Still, she doesn't have to take it out on other people."

"Really, she's a lot of fun when you get to know her," Katie said loyally. "It's just that she has a flair for the dramatic. She's in lots of school plays, and even did summer stock at the our local theater last year. *Annie.* She was Annie's understudy. She was going to be Annie, until, well . . . you know Rusty? The dog? Well, Jenna accidentally stepped on his tail. Every time she got near him, he hid under the director's chair and howled."

"I can sympathize."

"Trust me," Jenna said. "You guys are going to be great friends. Everyone likes Jenna. She was sixth grade class president."

Melissa rolled her eyes. "I'll bet she stuffed the ballot box."

"Two warnings, though. One, never, ever, not if your life depends on it, ask her to play her saxophone. I still have nerve damage in my right ear from 'Twinkle, Twinkle.' And two, don't let her talk you into something you'll regret. She has this nose for trouble. Her whole locker's wallpapered with detention slips."

"I've never gotten a detention slip," Melissa said. She almost sounded embarrassed. "I've never even missed a day of school."

"Well, don't hold that against Jenna. She'll grow on you."

"So do warts," Melissa said. "Anyway, I'm glad we ended up in the same tent, Katie. Jenna, I'm not so sure about."

Just then Rose came in, followed by Gary Stone, the vet who was married to Margaret, and a couple of the stablehands. Rose went to the front of the group and the room began to quiet. "Sorry I'm late, gang," she said. "But good things come to those who wait."

As Rose introduced the staff, Katie watched as J.T., one of the stablehands, approached Sharon's table. His eyes lingered on her, then ever so subtly dropped to her braces. He met Sharon's eyes for a split second before veering toward another table. She gave a nearly imperceptible shrug.

Katie sighed. Their tent had all the makings of a disaster: Jenna pouting, Sharon silent, and Jenna and Melissa already bickering. Not to mention a pile of goat turds. It was not a promising start.

Good things come to those who wait, she repeated silently. She hoped Rose was right.

"Welcome to Silver Creek," Rose said. "Your home away from home for this glorious summer."

Jenna shook her head. Rose was such a ham. Of course, it took one to know one, as they said.

"We have some of the finest horses and the finest instructors in the country, right here under our humble roof," Rose continued. "Some of the finest riders, too."

Jenna glanced over at Katie and Melissa. She felt like a jerk, taking out her anger about Turbo on innocent bystanders, but everyone seemed to be conspiring to remind her of him. Big surprise. She'd *told* Katie coming here would be a mistake.

She listened absently while Rose introduced the riding teachers and resident advisers, counselors who would be assigned to each tent. Jenna knew all the teachers, of course. In fact, she knew Silver Creek Stables inside out. She wasn't like some of the other riders, the ones who just showed up once a week and disappeared. Jenna came here every chance she got, just watching and learning.

"You'll find everything you'll need here at Silver Creek," Rose said. "We own hundred and forty acres, and Silver Creek meanders right through the middle of them. Our grounds are adjacent to Silver Creek State Park, as some of you know, which boasts glorious riding trails, not to mention spectacular bass fishing on Silver Lake. As for the stables, our little corner of heaven has an indoor ring, a dressage ring, a jumping arena, two training rings, a cross-country course, and, of course, miles and miles of beautiful trails. Then, of course, there are our beautiful horses. Each of you will be assigned a particular horse for the entire session. You will be responsible for all his care while you're here."

Foxy, Jenna thought. The horse she'd been riding for the past year, once Claire had decided that Jenna had her jumping skills up to par. They understood each other, she and Foxy. She was a tough old gal, strong-willed and spirited. Gorgeous, too. Not up to Turbo's high standards, of course, but still, Jenna loved her like she were her own horse.

Her own. The words sent an ache through her. She'd planned to bring Turbo here, to work on jumping and dressage in her spare time with Claire's help. He would have been great. Amazing.

"Now," Rose continued, "a typical day." She walked over to a little girl with black pigtails and a terrified smile. "You. What's your name?"

"Julie." It was barely a whisper.

"Well, Julie," Rose said, "what would you think the very first thing an average camper would do here at Silver Creek to start an average camper day?"

Julie's eyes darted around nervously. "Um, pee?"

Rose let out her hearty laugh, a laugh that could start an earthquake. "Okay, darling. After this typical Silver Creek camper visits the little filly's room, then what?"

Julie froze. "Um, cereal?" she ventured at last.

"Exactly!" Rose cried. "Cereal! But for who?"

"Me?" Julie tried.

"First, the horses, Julie! Here, the horses always come first! Everyone will be assigned to feed crew at some point during their stay. At six-thirty sharp the horses are grained and given light hay. From seven-thirty to eight, the rest of us are grained. Hay is optional." Rose laughed at her own joke. "Half hour for tent cleanup, and then it's straight to the stables to muck out stalls and clean and check tack. For those of you who haven't yet discovered the joys of mucking out a stall, trust me—you'll never feel closer to your horse."

Jenna glanced at Sharon. Would all this be hard for her? Caring for a horse required a lot of physical effort. Of course, Melissa had said that Sharon owned a horse. And Silver Creek wouldn't have admitted her to the camp if they didn't think she could handle it.

"Until eleven forty-five, you live and breathe horses," Rose continued. "Depending on your skill level, you'll be placed in a small class to work on horsemanship, jumping exercises, cavaletti work, or basic dressage routine. There'll be a half-hour cool-down—that's for your horse, not you—and then it's time for lunch." Rose turned back to Julie. "And who gets to eat first?"

"The horses!" Julie exclaimed, and several of the older campers applauded.

"Now, after lunch we give the horses a rest for an hour and a half. It's up to you how you spend your time, but there's plenty to keep you busy. We have a gorgeous lake for you to swim in or canoe on, and then there are the usual suspects—volleyball, softball, archery. There's also a wonderful art studio in a small converted farmhouse near the main barn where you can sculpt, paint, or sketch. Surprisingly enough, horses seem to be a popular subject, but I'm offering my undying gratitude to anyone who can capture the real me on paper for posterity."

Jenna looked over at Katie and Melissa, who were laughing at Rose, along with the rest of the campers. *What's wrong with me?* Jenna wondered. Why couldn't she get into the spirit of things? She'd been looking forward to this for months, and now all she could do was lick her wounds and feel sorry for herself.

No, she corrected, it wasn't just herself. It was Turbo. She was feeling sorry for him, too. Who knew what kind of owner he'd end up with? No one could possibly love him more than she would have.

"For those of you who aren't artistically inclined, we offer intensive seminars on other aspects of horse care." Rose ticked them off on her fingers. "Foal training, stable management, horse-show planning, veterinary care . . . you name it. At three o'clock we tack up again for afternoon group riding studies—trail riding, cross-country schooling, that sort of thing.

After cooling out, at five-thirty, the horses go back to their stalls, where they get to—" She paused, turning to Julie.

"Pee!" Julie cried in triumph as the room burst into laughter.

"Close enough, darling. After dinner, we'll have plenty of activities scheduled—games, bonfires, soccer nights, even dances. At nine-thirty the feed crews do a final barn check and night watering. Shortly thereafter, you all will fall promptly into bed, exhausted."

Rose adopted her drill sergeant look, the one that had sent shivers down Jenna's spine on more than one occasion. "Now," she continued, holding up a warning finger, "the no-nos. First and foremost, no mistreating the horses, ever. They are your number one priority. Also, no drugs, no alcohol, no smoking. No leaving the camp without prior permission. And although I'm sure I don't have to worry on this score, because I know most of you and the rest have been carefully screened so that we'll have only the most angelic of campers—no troublemaking. This covers a variety of sins. I'm not going to tell you what they are. It will only encourage you."

Rose eyeballed Jenna, who shifted uncomfortably. She had a reputation she really didn't deserve. Entirely, anyway.

As Rose droned on about the layout of the camp, Jenna's eyes strayed back to Sharon. It was hard not to wonder how she would do in the saddle during tryouts. She looked so lonely, sitting there by herself, that Jenna considered joining her. *After all*, she told herself, *misery loves company*. But when

Jenna caught her eye, Sharon stared right through her.

Forget Sharon, Jenna muttered under her breath. *I've got problems of my own.*

5

With a bridle over her shoulder and a saddle and pad over her right arm, Katie headed from the crowded tack room down the long sunny aisle to Say-So's stall.

After orientation, Rose had picked out several of the older, more experienced riders and asked them to tack up the horses so tryouts could begin. Katie wasn't exactly experienced, but she was glad for the chance to help out.

Down the aisle, she could hear Jenna carrying on a conversation with Foxy, the piebald mare she'd been riding all year. Melissa was in the stall next door, tacking up Trickster, the gray mare who was the best jumper in the stables. Rose had asked Sharon to help out, too, but Katie didn't see her anywhere.

"Hey, Say," Katie cooed. Say-So, a sweet-tempered bay gelding, pricked up his ears as she unlatched his stall door. He whuffled softly in her ear when she was close. She'd been riding Say ever since she'd started lessons at Silver Creek the beginning of last year, after Jenna had convinced her to come watch a lesson.

Up until then, riding had been one of the few things she and Jenna *hadn't* done together. It wasn't that Katie didn't love horses—she was a total animal freak and had a special place in her heart for hard-luck cases. She had a Manx cat named Beast that was not only missing his tail but his left hind leg as well (according to the animal shelter where she'd found him, he'd had a run-in with a riding mower). She had a big, sloppy mixed-breed dog named Beauty that was so arthritic she had to carry him up the stairs to her room each night. She also had two aquariums, four gerbils, a blind lizard she'd rescued from a neighborhood cat, and a tarantula that answered to the name of Charlotte and had an affection for corn dogs. Katie had read every animal book ever written, she was pretty sure. If her grades allowed it (a big if), she wanted to be a zoo vet someday, working to breed endangered species. When she was older, she was going to beg Gary for a chance to work in his office. No veterinary school would turn her down if she had hands-on experience like that!

She would have been a natural for riding, if it weren't for the fact that her brain and her body didn't always communicate in the same language. Jenna, on the other hand, was a natural athlete, star pitcher on her softball team, the first kid to have her training wheels removed, and, of course, a first-class rider. Katie *tried* not to hate her best friend for that, but it was tough sometimes.

"Ready for action, Say?" Katie asked. Gently she lifted the saddle above his withers and moved it into position, sliding it with the hair, then checking to be sure the pad was lying flat.

In the next stall, she could hear Melissa struggling to place the bit in Trickster's mouth.

"He's a little head-shy," Katie said. "Hang in there."

Melissa laughed. "I've seen worse, believe me. There was this Arabian at my last stable who used to throw his head up out of reach every time he saw you coming with a bridle. We finally outsmarted him by rubbing molasses on the bit. He loved it."

"Hey, who's tacking up Blooper?" Jenna called, nodding toward the big bay gelding in the stall next to Foxy's.

"I think Rose asked Sharon to," Katie said. She glanced up and down the stalls, but Sharon was nowhere in sight.

Katie reached for the girth and positioned it just behind Say-So's elbow, the way Margaret had taught her the day of her first class. She remembered how confused she'd felt, hearing the other riders speak what seemed like a foreign language. *Cavesson noseband. Cantle and pommel. Eggbutt snaffle bit.* She'd been thoroughly lost, trying to distinguish between the long strips of leather that crisscrossed the horse's head like a downtown road map. And she'd been frightened by the sheer size of all the horses, towering above her with those eyes that said *one wrong move and I could toss you off my back like a sack of flour.*

She had fallen in the ring a few times, of course. Nothing bruised beyond her rear and her ego. Katie knew that everyone fell, that everyone had bad days riding, but sometimes she wondered if she'd ever be the kind of rider Jenna and Melissa were.

Still, she couldn't imagine *not* riding. She loved being around the horses too much. She loved trying to crawl inside their heads and figure out what they were thinking. Was it *ease up on the reins, you jerk* or maybe *I'll love you forever if you just scratch that place right behind my left ear*? You had to think like a horse did.

When she'd secured Say's girth, Katie decided to check on Sharon. She found her alone in the large, neatly organized tack room, a bridle slung over her shoulder. Sharon was staring at the long row of empty tiered saddle racks, hands on her hips, her mouth drawn into a flat line.

"You'd think this place would have enough saddles," she muttered. "Can't anyone here count?"

Louisa Tisch, a thin, bubbly eighth grader with a nervous giggle who'd been in Katie's riding class all spring, bounced into the room. "Where are the extra hard hats? I've looked all over and I can't—"

Katie pointed to the shelf behind her. "Right there, Louisa," she said, "where they always are."

"Oh, right. I'm such an airhead." Louisa turned to Sharon. Her eyes plummeted to the floor. "Um, hi," she said in a fluttery voice, her gaze welded to Sharon's braces. "I'm Louisa."

"Um, hi," Sharon said flatly. "I'm crippled."

Louisa's cheeks flooded with color. "Sharon," Katie began, "you shouldn't—"

"Sorry, Katie," Sharon said. "I meant, I'm differently abled. Better?"

Katie waited. She had the feeling Sharon was trying to make her uncomfortable. "About those saddles," Katie said. "I think Rose said she sent a couple over to Saddle Up in Pooleville for repairs. See that door over by the leg wraps? There's a little storage area upstairs and there might be a spare saddle up there. I'll go check."

"I'll go," Sharon said.

"But—" Louisa began. She flashed a look at Katie. "I mean, saddles are heavy, and with the stairs and all, you can't—"

Sharon smiled at Louisa. It wasn't a nice smile, Katie realized. It wasn't quite like any smile she'd ever seen.

"Well," Louisa said, grabbing several hard hats, "I guess I'll be, um . . . nice meeting you."

Sharon opened the door to the storage area and slowly made her way up the stairs. A minute later she came back down carrying a saddle in her arms, navigating each stair with care.

Suddenly Katie realized she was doing just what Louisa had been doing—staring at Sharon's braces. "If there's anything else you can't find," she said, quickly looking away, "let me know."

She returned to Say-So's stall and led him out. Jenna and Melissa were just about finished. "Should one of us tack up Blooper?" Jenna asked.

Katie shook her head. "Sharon's coming."

Just then Sharon appeared, walking heavily down the long aisle.

"Let me help you," Jenna called. "If you want, I can saddle up Blooper."

Sharon paused before the bay's stall. "Blooper," she said. "Hmm. I wonder if I should read some significance into that?"

She unlatched his door and headed inside. Melissa looked at Katie. "Shouldn't we—"

"No," Katie answered. "I guess we shouldn't."

• • •

Sharon checked Blooper's girth and sighed. She was tired already. Everything, *everything*, was harder now. Not that she could admit it to anyone.

While she was recovering in the hospital, both legs in casts up to her thighs, they'd made her go to a support group for people with disabilities. There were three other car accident victims, plus a seventh grader with bone cancer who'd had half his leg amputated and a girl in college who'd been paralyzed when she'd fallen off a third-floor balcony after drinking half a pack of beer.

Except for Sharon, they were all model patients. Sure, they got depressed sometimes, but nobody seemed angry, not the way that Sharon was angry. Only Sharon had thrown lime Jell-O at a nurse. Only Sharon had reduced a candy striper to tears. And only Sharon swore to anyone who would listen that she was going to be one hundred percent okay again.

The day she left the hospital, Courtney, the paralyzed girl, had wheeled into her room just as Sharon was getting ready to leave. Sharon had talked about riding again, about how she couldn't wait to get back in the saddle once she was done with rehab.

Courtney had looked at her and smiled. "You don't get it, do you? You can't go back to who you were."

"The nerve damage isn't that bad," Sharon had said. "They'll take the steel rod out of my left leg in a few months and after a little therapy—"

"That's not what I meant. I *meant* you're not the same *inside* anymore. Even if your legs were a hundred percent, you're not who you were, Sharon."

Sharon rubbed her cheek against Blooper's thick mane. He was a good old guy, docile as a baby lamb, and probably just about as much fun to ride. Cassidy, he wasn't.

She'd already done some riding at the rehab center nearby called PET—Program for Equestrian Therapy. That's where she'd met Claire Donovan, who was a volunteer there. Claire was the one who'd arranged the scholarship to Silver Creek's summer program, even though Sharon had quit after a few rounds at the rehab center. It had bored her, walking and trotting in tight little circles like a kid on a carnival pony. She needed more, a lot more. She needed to *really* ride.

Courtney was wrong. Sharon *was* the same person. Her legs were a little weak. She was a little out of practice in the saddle. But she was still Sharon Finnerty, championship rider.

Even if, for the moment, her mighty steed just happened to be named Blooper.

By the time Sharon led Blooper outside, the campers had already been divided into two groups. Beginners were in the smaller training ring with Margaret and three other teachers. More experienced riders were in the larger ring adjacent to the main barn. One at a time, Claire asked each rider to execute a figure eight at a walk, a sitting trot, and a posting trot. Advanced riders were also required to do a figure eight at a canter with a flying change of leads. All things Sharon could do in her sleep . . . at least in the old days.

Sharon stood at the edge of the group, holding Blooper's reins while he sniffed at her hair, which was, as usual, whipping in the breeze like a red flag. She watched with a critical eye as Jenna and Melissa rode. They were both good, among the top riders, although they had very different styles. Melissa was a cool, intellectual rider, sheer grace to watch. Jenna may have lacked some of Melissa's classical form, but she made up for it with an energetic confidence that sent a rush through Sharon. That's the kind of rider she had been . . . *That's the kind of rider I still am*, she reminded herself.

Katie was next. She mounted Say-So easily, but you could see the anxiety in her eyes. Sharon knew it well, the top-of-the-roller-coaster moment when you were pumped up on adrenaline like a balloon about to burst. She remembered her first show, nearly seven years ago. She'd been a nervous wreck, much like Katie looked now as she tried to change diagonals.

Sharon had won a blue ribbon at that first show, and she'd never felt those nerves again. Not until now.

Katie finished and walked Say-So out. "Nice job," Claire said reassuringly, but Katie just rolled her eyes.

Another counselor glanced down at her clipboard. "Sharon Finnerty?"

Sharon led Blooper through the crowd to the open gate. Was it just her imagination or had the group suddenly gotten suspiciously quiet?

Claire was waiting for her in the ring. "You know, you could have given me a horse with a little more spirit, Claire," Sharon chided. "This isn't exactly Secretariat."

"Just do what you can," Claire said, giving her a warning look that said *don't get carried away*. Sharon

knew. She'd seen it before, at the rehab center. Claire
was the same height as Sharon, thin, with curly dark
hair and light blue eyes the color of a clear morning sky.
She didn't *look* particularly intimidating, but Sharon
knew better. She'd seen Claire ride.

Sharon winked at Blooper. "Do me a favor, guy,"
she whispered, "and don't live up to your name."

This was the part she'd been dreading. Mounting
put the most strain on her left leg, the one that had
been badly crushed in the accident. At the equestrian
rehab center she'd used a mounting ramp, and later
she'd had one of the volunteers give her a leg up. She'd
done it the right way just a few times since then. It
hurt like crazy.

She gathered up her reins in her left hand, keeping
a light contact with Blooper's mouth, and grabbed a
lock of his mane in front of the saddle. In the old
days, she'd practically flown into the saddle, but now
she needed all the help she could get, and she knew
there were few nerve endings at the root of the mane.
It wouldn't hurt Blooper; it might help her.

She twisted the stirrup iron a quarter turn clock-
wise. Now came the hard part. With her right hand
under her thigh as a sort of power assist, she lifted
her leg toward the stirrup. On her second try, she
managed to get her specially made boot centered in it.

Claire came closer. "Am I holding up the works?"
Sharon asked.

"Of course not. You want a leg up?"

"Of course not."

One, two, three bounces on her right foot, her
right hand on the cantle, and Sharon hefted herself
up. Halfway there, her left foot gave out, slipping out

of the stirrup. She slid back to the ground, landing heavily on both legs. Lightning bolts of pain shot up her bones. But wincing was out of the question. Instead Sharon gave the crowd a gritted-teeth grin.

She heard people whispering, that concerned *tut-tut* noise she hated. Sharon looked over at her tentmates. Melissa was chewing on her lower lip. Jenna was giving her an atta-girl grin. When Katie saw Sharon looking her way, she gave her a small, barely perceptible nod of encouragement.

"Sharon—" Claire said softly.

Sharon glared at her.

"All right, all right." Claire held up her hands. "Let it not be said that I can't take a hint."

Sharon repositioned herself. The whispering picked up, like a rush of wind through a dry field.

"For those of you taking bets," Sharon said loudly, "the current odds are five to two I fall flat on my face."

The whispering stopped. Sharon eased her foot back into the stirrup and, with a grunt of effort, hoisted herself up and over in one fluid movement.

A few people gasped. Some smiled. Some still looked doubtful. Sharon glanced over at Katie. Katie nodded again. She, for one, didn't look at all surprised.

Sharon started Blooper in a walk around the ring, letting her tight thigh and calf muscles warm up before nudging him behind the girth with her left leg to send him into a nice, easy trot. He was no Derby winner, she'd been right about that, but he had a smooth enough trot, and she began to relax as she felt the familiar two-beat gait beneath her.

She started to post, rising as Blooper's outside shoulder moved forward. But as she rose, she had to tighten her knees and put more weight into her stirrups and heels. Unfortunately, her weak left knee wasn't cooperating. It started to give way, and she had to drop into the saddle early, losing her rhythm and confusing Blooper.

She sat for a couple beats and tried again. This time wasn't much of an improvement. Her lower legs were weak, and her left foot in particular had a way of slipping out of the stirrup when she least expected it. Just when she finally seemed to have talked her legs into behaving, it was time to change diagonals, and she was back to square one.

It was as if some of her muscles had lost their memory. Part of her was still the skilled equestrian who could communicate with a horse with incredible precision and subtlety. But another part of her had turned into an awkward beginner. No wonder Blooper was having trouble reading her. It was as if he were carrying two different riders on his back. From the seat up, Sharon was one rider. From the thighs down, she was another.

Sharon finished and stopped Blooper near the gate. Dismounting was easier than mounting. She looked over at Claire, who was writing something on a notepad. "Good work, Sharon," she said.

"Yeah, right. Under the circumstances."

"It'll get easier," Claire said.

Sharon led Blooper away, away from the prying eyes, away from the scene of her failure. For a year and a half, people had been telling her things would get easier. She wondered when the easy part would finally begin.

6

"Claire, can we talk?" Katie asked quietly at dinner that evening.

Claire looked up from her tray of tacos. The din of laughter and clattering silverware echoed off the lodge walls. "Sure," she said. She scooched down on the bench and patted the empty spot. "Sit."

Katie hesitated. "No, it's . . . It'll only take a minute." Suddenly she regretted coming over to the counselors' table like this. She felt like a little kid invading the parents' table at Thanksgiving.

"Speak, Katie," Rose urged. "Could this perhaps be about the class placements we just posted?"

"How'd you know?" Katie asked. She felt her face begin to heat up. She had this annoying habit of blushing at the most inconvenient times.

"Well, you're only the hundred and thirteenth person to come over here and interrupt our taco consumption to complain."

"I'm sorry," Katie said. "I'll go—"

Claire grabbed her arm. "Don't you dare. Look, I know you're probably upset about me separating you

59

and Jenna for the morning class session."

Katie nodded. "It's just that we've been together in class all year—"

"But there are just eight students in your regular class, Katie." Claire frowned at a taco ingredient and tossed it aside with her fork. "Here at camp we have many more kids with varied skills. That means we can fine-tune the classes a little more. And don't forget that Jenna's been riding much longer than you have. This is no reflection on your skills. You're a fine rider. And you have great instincts with the horses."

"She's part horse, did you know that?" Rose said to a guy sitting at the next table, an eighth grader named Jake. Katie had noticed him around school. She doubted the reverse was true.

"She doesn't look it," Jake said, grinning.

Katie felt her blush creep down to her toes. "And besides," Claire continued, as if she'd already given this speech a few times, "you'll be together for most of the activities. Afternoon classes, the trail rides, the free time."

"I guess you're right," Katie said uncertainly.

"There comes a time when the bird has to leave the nest and try her wings," Rose said.

"So I'm the bird?"

"I thought you said she was part horse," Jake said.

"Katie's very versatile," Rose said confidently.

"Claire, can we talk?" Jenna asked.

Claire looked up from her fruit salad. "I don't suppose you're here to discuss world affairs? The state of the union? The economy, maybe?"

"I know all about the economy. No one has any

money, me especially." Jenna sat down on the edge of the bench and nudged Claire over.

"Please," Claire said, "sit down. I insist."

"There's no reason why you should give Melissa my horse. I've been riding Foxy all year. We understand each other."

"You understand each other too well." Claire picked at an unidentifiable brown item at the bottom of her fruit salad. "That's why I want you to ride Trickster for a while. She'll make a better rider out of you."

"What's that supposed to mean, 'better rider'?"

Rose turned to Jake. "Jenna's one of our more, shall we say, *vocal* campers."

"You're a great rider, Jenna," Claire said patiently. "I want you to be an even greater rider, to think with your head a little more and your gut a little less."

"I do not think with my gut," Jenna said irritably. "Which is a good thing, after that taco slop we just consumed."

Claire sighed. Jenna could tell she was on thin ice. Claire had a temper. She rarely showed it, but Jenna was one of the few campers who'd ever experienced its full force. She had a way of bringing that out in people.

"Look," Jenna said, softening her tone to a pleading whine. It never worked on her parents, but she was desperate. "I'm very vulnerable right now, Claire. Nothing's going the way I planned—"

"I was so sorry to hear about Turbo, dear," Rose said.

At the sudden gentleness in Rose's voice, tears flooded Jenna's eyes. "Fine," she said abruptly, leaping up. "I can see you're too busy with your fruit to listen to reason."

Behind her, she heard Claire ask, "What is this brown thingie, anyway? Has anyone checked the new cook's references?"

"Claire—"

"Sit."

Melissa hesitated. "Sorry," Claire apologized. "It's been a long meal." She poked at her strawberry shortcake. "So what have I done wrong?"

"Wrong?" Melissa asked. "Nothing. It's just that Jenna seems so mad about me riding Foxy that I thought maybe we could switch or something. I don't want her furious with me for the whole session. I mean, her cot's right across from mine. How am I supposed to get a good night's sleep? There's no telling what she's capable of."

Rose nodded. "Melissa has a fine grasp of human nature," she told Jake. She winked at Melissa. "You ride Foxy, dear. You've got the talent and experience to handle her. I knew when I saw you two together this morning you'd make a splendid pair."

"And don't worry about Jenna. She's got a lot on her mind," Claire said. "And her bark's worse than her bite. Usually." She dug through her shortcake as if she were mining for gold. After a moment, she pulled out a black lump with her fingers.

"Here," she said at last, shoving her plate at Melissa, "want my dessert?"

"No, we cannot talk," Claire said, sipping at her coffee, "unless you can do it without mentioning the word *horse* once."

"Fine. No problem," Sharon said. She crossed her

arms over her chest and glared at Claire. "Here goes. I realize I was not exactly up to championship form today, but what do you mean putting me into an intermediate class with a bunch of people who don't know a mane from a tail?"

Claire dropped her head on her arms.

"Be gentle with Claire," Rose advised. "She appears to be having a breakdown."

"And while we're at it," Sharon continued, "I went to check out the horse—oh, excuse me—the mammal of the equine persuasion—you assigned me—if you can call that bag of bones a—well, you know."

"Mind your tongue, now," Rose warned. "I saved Escape Route from being put down last year. He may be a little rusty, but so am I, dear girl, and trust me, we both have plenty of get-up-and-go left."

"Well, he's no Blooper," Sharon said sarcastically.

Claire raised her head. She cast a plaintive look at Rose. "Is there something in their water, maybe?"

"I'm serious, Claire. You know I'm a better rider than you're letting me be."

"Look," Claire said, lowering her voice, "what you know how to do and what you can do are two different things right now, Sharon. You've got to accept that. It may change—in fact, I'm sure it will. But in the meantime, you've got to take things slowly. Riding isn't just about competing, you know."

Sharon fell silent. She hated the condescension in Claire's voice, the tone she might use with a beginning six-year-old rider who wanted to canter before she could walk.

Claire took a last sip of coffee and stood. "There's something I've been meaning to talk to you about,

Sharon." She led her away from the table to a quiet corner. Already the lodge was emptying. Through the open window, Sharon heard the hollow bounce of a volleyball being served.

"The thing is," Claire said, "I've gotten in a little over my head on something, and I'm hoping you can help bail me out."

Sharon crossed her arms, waiting for the catch.

"There's this two-year-old filly I promised a friend I'd work on lunge training while camp's in session. She's a beauty, but she's going to be a handful. My friend bought her from another guy who tried to train her without knowing what he was doing, and now she's practically unmanageable. I really think he abused her. I'd planned to work with her on my off time, but I just found out we're going to be short a teacher this session, and I'm not going to have a lot of extra time."

"So?"

"So," Claire said, "you told me at the rehab center that you used to help your uncle break in horses while you were growing up in Vermont. I thought maybe I could talk you into giving me a hand with this filly."

"Is this your idea of throwing me a bone?" Sharon asked. "You can't ride anymore, Sharon, so why don't you do something else? Something that doesn't require a saddle?"

"That's not it at all, Sharon. I just thought, with your background—"

"I don't want to train somebody else's bratty filly."

"She's not bratty. She's afraid."

Sharon looked out the window, past the volleyball game and the feed barn and the trees. A hawk glided over the pines. No movement, just wings spread wide. Pure freedom.

"What is it you do want, Sharon?" Claire asked gently.

"What I want," Sharon said, "is to ride again, the way I used to. Free. Without thinking about it. Just doing it."

"I know." Claire followed Sharon's gaze. The hawk swooped and dipped, carried on currents only he could see. "It'll get easier, Sharon. It really will. You just have to be patient."

"Yeah. Patience." The hawk disappeared in a dark mass of pines. "Sorry I can't help you with the filly, Claire. I wouldn't be any good at it, anyway. You know me. Patience is the one thing I don't have."

"What's that you're reading, Katie?" Melissa asked.

Katie was sprawled out on her cot, reading a hardcover book. After dinner, the girls had returned to their tent, where their adviser was supposed to be meeting them.

"It's called *Horse Power*," Katie answered. "I love to read books about animal psychology, especially horses. I think it makes you a better rider if you try to understand what's going on inside a horse's mind."

"For example," Jenna said as she propped two Polaroids on her dresser, "a horse can become very irritable if his usual rider is suddenly replaced by someone else."

"Jenna, I tried to talk to Claire about Foxy," Melissa said. She didn't want Jenna angry with her. By the same token, she didn't really see why Jenna was making such a fuss. Stable horses had to adjust to lots of different riders—and stable riders had to adjust to lots of different horses.

"Do we have to fill this place with all these Kodak memories?" asked Sharon, who was brushing her hair in quick, urgent strokes. "I thought people came to camp to get away from home."

Melissa rolled her eyes. Sharon had been grumbling ever since dinner.

"It's my dresser, I'll decorate it my way," Jenna replied. "Look at Katie. She's got stuff everywhere."

Sharon put down her brush and carefully side-stepped Katie's open trunk, which was overflowing with art supplies, photos, sketches, books, and jumbled clothes. "Not bad," Sharon said, examining a drawing of a bright-eyed gerbil. "A relative?"

"That's Floyd. I taught him to put a paper basket-ball through a hoop for my science project this year."

"You must lead a very full life." Sharon peered into Katie's trunk. "You actually brought a first-aid kit?"

"Katie's always prepared for the worst," Jenna said. "She's the only girl in junior high who carries a complete sewing kit in her purse."

"Suppose your hem goes out?" Katie said.

Sharon nodded. "Suppose you need to perform an emergency appendectomy?"

"Don't pick on Katie," Melissa said, rising to her defense. "I packed a lot, too, just to be on the safe side." She held up the big flashlight she'd brought, carefully labeled with her name, home address, and telephone number. "And I labeled everything."

"Everything?" Sharon repeated.

"Your toothbrush?" Jenna asked.

Melissa nodded.

"Your underwear?"

"It said to in the letter to campers. Didn't you read it?"

"I lost mine," Katie admitted.

"What letter?" Sharon asked indifferently.

Jenna narrowed her eyes. "You're very organized, aren't you, Melissa?"

"Well, I try—"

Katie laughed. "You're one to talk, Jenna."

"At least I don't label my underwear," Jenna said.

Katie grinned at Melissa. "Jenna just likes to organize *other* people. Besides, I happen to know she owns a complete set of days-of-the-week underwear."

"Some people just check their calendars," Sharon pointed out.

A tense silence fell. Melissa leaned back against her pillow and gazed at her photo of her old friends back home. What was wrong with everyone? Katie seemed genuinely nice, but Jenna and Sharon weren't exactly making things easy. She wondered if their bad moods had anything to do with her.

Make it work, Melissa. She'd promised herself.

"Jenna," she asked, "who's that in that picture?"

"My sister. Allegra."

"And the other one, of the beautiful horse? Who's he belong to?"

"He *should* have belonged to me." Jenna fell back on her cot and stared at the ceiling.

Melissa sighed. One down, one to go. She turned to Sharon. "Sharon, did you happen to bring a picture of Cassidy? She's such a beautiful horse, I thought Katie and Jenna might like to see what she—"

"No." Sharon spat out the word.

Fine. She'd tried. Melissa turned back to her computer, where she'd been composing a letter to Marcus. *I'm trying*, she typed. *But this is never going to work.*

For a while, no one spoke. Finally Katie broke the silence. "Know what? It says here that some stallions will only mate with mares of a certain color. They think it has something to do with the color of the stallion's mother. He imprints on her coat color and follows her around, and then later that color preference stays with him. Weird, huh? I mean, that horses could actually show color prejudice?"

"Not so weird," Melissa said. "People do it all the time." She was surprised by the anger in her own voice.

Katie looked up sharply. Understanding dawned on her face. "Not all people," she said.

One of my tentmates seems okay, Melissa typed. *Katie. But the other two . . .*

"I like your stuffed horse," Katie said.

Melissa looked up from her laptop. Katie nodded at the little black horse on Melissa's pillow.

At least Katie was trying.

"My boyfriend gave it to me before I moved here," Melissa said.

"Do you miss him a lot?"

"We talked every night after we moved, until my mom got the first long-distance bill and hit the roof. So now we mostly just write. Sometimes we even fax each other on our computers."

Katie smiled wistfully. "High-tech romance."

"Do you have a boyfriend, Katie?"

"Me?" Katie flushed, then laughed. "No way."

"Way," Jenna muttered.

"Well, there *is* one guy at school who's been flirting with me. At least I think he's been flirting with me."

"What are the symptoms?" Melissa asked.

"Well, whenever he's around me he blushes a lot, he winks at me, he trips, he sweats—"

"Sounds like the swine flu," Sharon offered.

"That's why I read romances," Katie confided. "I keep thinking I'll pick up some pointers."

"You want pointers, stick with your books on animal behavior," Sharon advised.

Jenna rolled onto her side. "How old are you, anyway, Sharon?"

"Fourteen."

"So you're going into ninth grade this fall?"

"Eighth." Sharon looked away. "I lost some time last year."

"I'll be in eighth, too," Melissa said. "How about you, Katie?"

"Seventh. Jenna, too."

"I suppose that makes me the elder stateswoman of the group," Sharon said.

"I guess you've probably had—" Katie hesitated, "lots of boyfriends."

"Me? Hundreds. Truckloads. I'm especially in demand as a dance partner."

Again the tent fell silent. Outside, laughter carried on the wind like bird songs. *We get started, then someone says something wrong and we fall apart*, Melissa thought. Like a balloon that begins to rise, then sinks under its own weight.

She wondered about Sharon. What had happened to her? Was there a way she could ask, gently? Maybe she'd feel better talking about it. But no. Sharon didn't seem like the type who wanted to talk about much of anything.

A shadow blocked the dusky light at the tent flap. "Knock, knock, Thoroughbreds!" came a bright voice. A very tall girl with very short brown hair entered briskly. "Hello, all," she said. "I'm your tent adviser." She took a little bow. "First, my name. It's pronounced *Danielle*, but I like to leave out the extra *le* at the end." She pointed to her name tag. "Well, I guess that's obvious."

"Wouldn't that make you *Daniel*, as in a guy's name?" Jenna asked. "Or am I missing something?"

Daniel settled on the edge of Sharon's cot. "I just got tired of writing those extra letters all the time, you know? Now, let me see if I've got my happy campers straight." She pointed with a finely manicured fingernail. "Sharon, Katie, Jenna, Melissa. Right?"

Melissa nodded. "What exactly does a tent adviser do?"

"Well, I'm here if you need me, as a guide, a counsel, a shoulder to cry on." She gazed at them speculatively. "Any of you having personal problems? Nervous about your classes? Dysfunctional families?"

"Well, I was feeling a little uncomfortable about Jenna and me being separated," Katie admitted. "We're best friends, and we've always taken lessons here at Silver Creek together—"

"You'll be fine, Katie," Jenna said. "You won't even miss me."

Melissa was surprised at the way Jenna's voice had suddenly softened. Was it possible Jenna actually had a *nice* side?

"See?" Daniel said. "All settled. So Katie was upset about being in a different class." She looked at Sharon meaningfully. "Anyone else want to share?"

"I'm upset you're on my cot," Sharon said.

Daniel rose uncomfortably. "Anything else we need to discuss as a tent unit?"

"Yeah." Jenna sat up. "The origins of the universe."

"We did that at lunch," Sharon said. "How about the nature of time and space?"

Daniel rubbed her hands together. "Well, we can deal with that another time, maybe. Now it's time for horse charades."

"Horse charades?" Melissa repeated.

"It's like regular charades, only you spell out things that have to do with horses. All the campers get together in the lodge. It's a riot."

Sharon groaned. "Is this an optional riot?"

"Come on," Daniel urged. "It's a great way to get to know your fellow campers."

"Were you by any chance a cheerleader in a former life, Daniel?" Sharon asked.

"Junior varsity two years, varsity one." Daniel executed a perfect split between cots.

Sharon pursed her lips. "Maybe we could all chip in and have you deprogrammed."

"Hey," Melissa said. "You have something against cheerleading?"

"Not you, too?"

"For two years," Melissa said proudly. "It's great aerobic exercise. And what's wrong with promoting school spirit?"

"There you go!" Daniel said, casting a relieved smile at Melissa. "Or camp spirit, for that matter? Now, before

we head on to the charades, there's some business I
need to take care of. Just for fun, we like to have a sort
of friendly competition between the tents during the
session. You're rewarded points for winning various
events, and at the end, the best tent wins a trophy.
And so does their adviser."

"What kind of events?" Jenna asked.

"Lots of things. Fun stuff like the charades tonight.
Games with the horses. And cleanliness, of course.
Once a week we inspect the tents—nothing formal,
mind you. I mean, we're not the Marines. But the
cleanest tent gets added points." She scanned the tent
and sighed. "Of course, I won't hold my breath on that
one."

"I was working on something earlier today that
might help," Melissa said. "A chart of duties for us to
follow." She pulled up the chart on her laptop screen.

"What duties?" Jenna demanded. "We're here to
ride horses, Melissa."

"I think a chart's a wonderful idea," Daniel said.

"Inspired," Sharon agreed flatly.

"I was going to list all our classes," Melissa said,
"so we'd know where everybody was at any time. That
sort of thing."

"Well, I like the idea," Katie offered. "Since, as you
can probably tell, I'm not the most organized person
on earth."

"I don't need anyone to tell me what to do or where
to be," Jenna said irritably.

"Did you ever consider Jenna with one n?" Sharon
interrupted. "Think of the time you'd save—"

Daniel stood abruptly, hands on hips. "In a few days
we're going to be going on our first trail overnight—"

"Trail overnight?" Katie repeated nervously. "I've never been on an overnight before."

"You'll love it," Melissa assured her.

"I think I'll pass on that," Sharon announced. "I prefer these wonderfully comfy cots."

"Passing is *not* an option," Daniel said. "We'd lose tent points. Which brings me to an urgent issue. I think you girls should know something." Her voice had turned brittle, like taffy hardening. "I know I shouldn't say this and it isn't good for morale, but, to be perfectly honest, nobody wanted your tent."

"Why?" Katie asked, staring at the ceiling. "Is there something wrong with it?"

"Not the *tent*," Daniel growled. "None of the advisers wanted the *people* in the tent." She took a deep breath, trying to compose herself. "You have, well, a reputation."

"All right!" Sharon cried. "And on our first day, too. Way to go, little campers."

"A reputation as disruptive, argumentative, and, well . . ."

"Outlaws?" Sharon offered. "Rebels?"

"Hooligans?" Jenna suggested.

Daniel lowered her voice to a whisper. "As much as it pains me to say this, I overheard one counselor refer to you as 'those little boogers.' "

"No," Jenna cried, flinging her hand to her forehead. "Not the *B*-word!"

Daniel sighed. "That's not the worst of it. I'm sorry to tell you this, girls, but they're already calling your tent the 'Thoroughbrats.' " She headed for the door flap. "Now, I'm going to go have some charades fun. Speaking as your adviser, I hope you all will come and prove the rest of them wrong. It's time for you girls to think about bonding."

"Hmm," Sharon said when Daniel was gone. "Thoroughbrats. I kind of like the sound of it."

Melissa erased her screen. There was no point in trying to get organized. It would be enough just to survive.

Marcus, she typed. *Get me out of here!*

7

"What's a three-syllable horse name?" Katie asked. She and Melissa climbed up onto the fence surrounding an outdoor training ring. Claire was in the center, working with a dapple gray filly attached to a lunge line made of nylon webbing. In her right hand Claire held a six-foot-long lunging whip.

"First syllable sounds like *leg*," Melissa added.

Claire turned. "Give up on charades already?"

"We know, we know." Melissa shrugged. "We have an attitude problem."

"We're the Thoroughbrats, Claire," Katie said. "Haven't you heard?"

"Heard? I came up with the name."

"At least you didn't call us little boogers."

"Don't be too sure."

"Whoa," Claire commanded as she tried to ease the horse to a stop. The filly jerked forward, tossing her head angrily, before finally relenting and coming to an uneasy halt.

"Atta girl." Claire led the horse over with difficulty. "Actually, you two aren't the booger constituency," she said, wiping her damp forehead with the back of her arm. "It's your tentmates who are the problem. Where are they, anyway?"

"Back in the tent, pouting."

"That would figure."

"Jenna's just disappointed about Turbo, that's all," Katie said.

"I know how much she had her heart set on him." Claire nodded. "But it's not like Jenna to be so down. Are you sure that's all that's going on? Family stuff, maybe? Her period?"

"I'm thinking she's possessed by the devil," Melissa offered. "But then, we just met."

"Intriguing theory," Claire said. She reached over to stroke the horse's neck, but she recoiled at Claire's touch. "Now if we could just figure out what to do about Sharon. I asked her if she'd help me out with Luna here, but she wasn't having any part of it. She thought I was just trying to take her mind off Cass, but the truth is, I really need some help with this gal."

"What do you mean, 'take her mind off Cass'?" Melissa asked.

"She didn't tell you?" Claire sighed. "No, knowing Sharon, I guess she wouldn't."

"Something happened to Cassidy?" Melissa pressed.

"I don't know. Maybe I should leave this for Sharon to tell." Claire shook her head. "But I suppose you'll hear about it sooner or later. About a year and a half ago, back when Sharon still lived in Vermont, she was riding on this back road when some punks in a truck—drunk, naturally—piled into them. Cass died right there."

"Oh, my God," Katie whispered.

"Sharon was in the hospital for months, and in rehab a lot longer. Her family moved here in January when her dad was transferred."

"I wonder why we never saw her at school?" Katie asked.

"Last I heard, she was going to Breton Academy," Claire said.

"That's a private school near Pooleville," Katie explained to Melissa.

"Anyway, I met Sharon at PET, the hippotherapy class I volunteer with."

"Hippotherapy?" Melissa repeated.

"It's this program where people with disabilities ride horses with the aid of volunteers," Claire said. "We only use specially trained horses." She gave Luna a frustrated look. "Calm, sweet-tempered horses— unlike *certain* gray fillies I know, who shall remain nameless. Not to mention riderless."

Claire leaned against the rail. "Anyway, the theory is, the movement of the horse, even at a slow walk, helps work muscle groups the person might not have control over. And it's great for them to be around the animals, of course. Sharon's rehab therapist talked her into coming to PET. It was the first time she'd been around horses in a year."

"And she started riding again?" Katie asked.

"Well, yes and no. She rode, all right. And of course she was capable of a lot more than the other people at the center. But that wasn't good enough, I guess. She wasn't the Sharon Finnerty who was on her way to the Olympics someday."

"She could have been that good," Melissa said quietly. "She really could have."

"So," Claire continued, "the moral of the story is, Sharon quit after a few sessions. I'd told her about Silver Creek and said I thought we could work out a scholarship, but I was kind of surprised to see her application in the mail."

"To lose your horse that way . . ." Katie's voice trailed off.

"She was a beautiful horse, too," Melissa said. "They made such a great team."

"I wish we could help Sharon somehow," Katie said.

"I've tried everything," Claire said wearily. "I think she just needs time. Keep an eye on her in class, Katie. You two will be together in the mornings."

"Like she's going to take pointers from me."

"You're a good rider, Katie. I know you're used to having Jenna around, but it'll do you good to be on your own. Anyway, maybe you can get through to Sharon. I sure can't." She sighed. "Of course, I can't even get through to Luna here. I really thought Sharon might be able to help me with her. Her uncle in Vermont had a farm, and she helped him break a lot of horses. Oh, well. The best-laid plans of mice and women . . ." She tightened her lunge line. "I gotta get back to work. By the way, Pegasus."

Katie frowned.

"The charades question. But don't tell 'em I told you guys. You're in enough trouble already."

Katie and Melissa walked back past the stable. "I feel so bad for Sharon," Katie said. "I wish there were something we could say."

"Like what? *Sorry your life got totally screwed up. Wanna go play horse charades?*"

"She'd feel better if she talked about it."

"That's what my mom's always telling me," Melissa said dismissively. "But what's talk got to do with it? After she and my dad divorced, she tried to get me to go to this support group for kids from broken-up families. They had these foam bats we were supposed to hit things with to take out our repressed anger. You know, perfectly harmless, no one gets hurt. The counselor kept saying, hit something, Melissa, you'll feel better. No way, I told her, I don't have any repressed anger, but she kept ragging on me, so finally I take a swing with the stupid bat." Melissa smiled faintly. "I broke a stained-glass lamp worth six hundred dollars."

"How'd you manage that?"

"I guess I unrepressed my anger, after all."

They walked past the lodge, where charades was still in full swing. "My parents divorced three years ago," Katie said. "My dad remarried last year."

"Who do you live with?"

"Him and my stepmom. Rae's her name."

Melissa seemed surprised. "Didn't your mom want you?"

"Of course she *wanted* me. But she's a photojournalist. She travels all over the world."

Melissa whistled. "Cool job."

"Yeah. Cool." Katie's voice sliced the air.

"Whoa." Melissa made a time-out sign with her hand. "Is that repressed anger I hear? You know what you need, don't you?"

"I'm fresh out of foam bats."

"This is much better than foam." Melissa grabbed her arm. "Cracker Jack."

"Actually, there's a certain resemblance—"

"Hey, don't pick on my Cracker Jack. I have a very limited supply and I don't share with just anyone."

Katie laughed. "Except certain goats."

They veered along the path that led back to the tent camp. Both girls fell silent. "Are you thinking about Sharon?" Katie asked at last.

"I can't stop thinking about her. But I don't know how we can help her, if she doesn't want to be helped."

Katie didn't answer. She was imagining what it must feel like to watch an animal you loved die before your very eyes. And the more she thought about it, the more she realized she couldn't begin to know how to help Sharon, not in a million years.

Sharon's journal
Day 8
I had it again, the same dream. I screamed so loud I think I woke half the ward. It was just like the other times. I'm at this major show and everyone's there, I mean *everyone*. The Pope, the Queen, the President, my junior high vice-principal—everyone.

It's a beautiful day. The sun's a white ball overhead. I'm wearing my favorite lucky hair ribbon. I'm on Cassidy and it's our final class, Junior Jumper. We're tooling around the arena, no sweat, having a perfect round. No faults, absolutely clean. I mean, Cassidy's sailing over those jumps like a Cessna and I'm just along for the ride.

I'm sure we've got it sewn up, if we can just clear the huge triple bar near the end of the course, the jump I know Cassidy hates. It's a killer, a widespread fence made of three sets of poles built in a staircase fashion, with the highest at the back.

As we approach the triple I tell her she can handle it. *That's my baby*, I say, *it's going to be okay*. I fold my body forward, we get deep into the fence and she gathers up all her power and takes this incredible leap. She trusts me, she knows if I say it's okay it will be.

But as we soar through the air, the triple disappears. It's vanished completely. I look down frantically, and then I know.

In its place is a beat-up sky-blue Ford.

I urge Cassidy on, I give her more rein. But no matter how high we go, no matter how far, that truck just keeps bearing down on us. I can see the drunken face of the driver, and I know he can see my fear. And all of a sudden I know we're going to hit the truck.

"There's something I have to tell you, Cass," I say, and then, like always, I'm screaming and the nurses are grabbing me and I wake up knowing it's too late. It will always be too late.

One of the nurses told me it's probably just the medication I'm taking, that it makes people have dreams, but I don't think so. Not like this one.

Sharon closed her journal and shivered. She'd been right about the medication. It hadn't been the painkillers that had made her have that dream. She'd had it a hundred times since that night in the hospital. A hundred and one, if you counted tonight.

She flicked off Melissa's big flashlight. Bugs were swarming to her hopefully. It was chilly out here by the lake. She was glad for her sweatshirt.

She heard the hiss of parting grass. "Sharon?"

Sharon flicked on the flashlight. Someone shaded her eyes. "What is that, a laser?"

It was Katie. Sharon sighed. Was there no escape from her tentmates?

"Did I wake you or something?" Sharon slipped her journal under her sweatshirt.

"That's okay. I'm kind of a night owl." Katie tucked her hair behind her ear. Her face was dotted with Clearasil. "I love it out here at night," she said. "It's like the animals get to take back the world."

She listened for a moment. Frogs complained loudly. Off in the stables, a horse whinnied. A fish jumped, shattering the smooth lake mirror. "Hear that? Bass, I'll bet."

"I like my fish quiet. Preferably with lemon butter." Sharon stood with difficulty. Katie held out her hand, then withdrew it.

"Well, that's about all the communing with nature I can stand for one night," Sharon said. "Sorry I woke you."

"Sharon?"

"Yeah?"

"Were you having a . . . you know, a bad dream? I thought maybe I heard you crying or something."

Wonderful. She was going to have to learn how to sleep with a pillow over her head. "Actually," Sharon said, "I've been having this recurring nightmare that I'm stuck in this big old tent that smells of goat farts with a bunch of strangers who won't leave me alone."

Even in the darkness, Sharon could see she'd hurt Katie. She felt a twinge of guilt, like a phantom pain, but it evaporated. It was just as well to send a clear message right off the bat.

"You'll get used to it," Katie said at last.

"No, I won't. I'm a very private person, okay?" Sharon's anger seemed to fill the night. "And I don't need strangers hovering over me, feeling sorry for me."

Katie gave a sliver of a smile, like the moon hovering above the fir trees. "Actually," she said with a shrug, "I was talking about the goat farts."

8

Jenna's eyes popped open. She pulled her pillow over her head to drown out the noise pouring through the tent flaps.

". . . unless the horse is the famous Mr. Ed!"

"Somebody wake me," Jenna groaned. "I'm dreaming I'm trapped in some ancient TV rerun."

"You're not dreaming." Katie's voice came from the other side of the tent. "That's the loudspeaker over at the lodge. Claire told me that's how they do morning wake-ups here. You know, instead of reveille?"

"I like it," Melissa said. "It's how they wake the shuttle astronauts."

Jenna opened one eye and peered past her pillow. "What *is* that yellow stuff?"

"It's called sunlight," said Melissa, who was sitting on her neatly made cot staring at her laptop computer. She was wearing a pair of shiny riding boots, beige jodhpurs, and a Baltimore Orioles T-shirt that looked like it had been starched and ironed.

"You're dressed," Jenna said accusingly.

Melissa looked up from her computer. "What, is that a crime or something?"

"Jenna's not a morning person," Katie explained.

In the other corner, Sharon groaned. "Morning," Melissa called.

Sharon moved slightly. "Unnhh."

"At least we know she's alive," Melissa said. "Come on, guys, let's get in gear."

"Do you have to be so . . . so perky?" Jenna growled.

Melissa looked at Katie. "Does she have to be so . . . so obnoxious?"

"Yeah, pretty much." Katie grinned. "During school I don't talk to her until second period. By then she can usually form complete sentences."

Sharon stirred. "Do you mind? I'm trying to get a little shut-eye over here."

"I wouldn't hang around in bed too long," Melissa warned. "I got the impression there's not all that much hot water in the showers to go around."

"I forgot," Katie said, digging through her trunk for shampoo. "We have to walk all the way back to the lodge to shower."

"It's not so bad," Melissa said. "Except for the part where all the guys can see you looking grungy."

"You, Ms. Starched T-shirt, grungy? I find that hard to believe," Jenna said.

"Thank you, Jenna," Melissa said icily. "I didn't know you cared."

"I can't go out like this!" Katie cried. "I have zit medicine all over my face."

"By the way, I already checked out the breakfast possibilities," Melissa added.

"I suppose you took Foxy out for a quick morning gallop, too," Jenna muttered.

Melissa ignored her. "The best candidate appears to be oatmeal. Although there's some weird-looking prune pudding stuff for the truly daring."

Jenna covered her face with her pillow.

"Unnnh," Sharon groaned again.

"Are we bonding yet?" Melissa asked.

By the time Jenna got to the stable after breakfast at the lodge, Melissa was already cantering around the ring with Foxy. Jenna paused to watch them take a low upright, followed by an oxer.

No doubt about it, Melissa was a good rider. Okay, a very good rider.

Okay, she rode like she'd been raised by horses.

Still, that didn't mean she didn't have some problems. All riders did. For example, she'd let Foxy stand off a bit, so that the horse had to stretch to get over the vertical. Of course, that just required a little work on her timing.

For another example, she just plain got on Jenna's nerves. And for that, there was no known cure.

"How're the Thoroughbrats?" Claire strode up behind Jenna.

"Well, there hasn't been any bloodshed, if that's what you mean."

"Good. It's so hard to get bloodstains out of tent canvas." She nodded at Melissa. "Good rider, huh?"

Jenna shrugged. "I suppose."

"You suppose right."

Jenna started toward the stable. "Are you just

trying to tick me off, Claire?" she asked over her shoulder.

"It's my life's mission," Claire said.

Jenna quickly grabbed her tack and went to Trickster's stall. The gray mare stared at her expectantly. Jenna stared back.

"I know," she said. "I usually ride Foxy. But Foxy's been horsenapped right from under my nose." She set down her saddle and ran her hand along Trickster's regal neck. "I can't seem to hang on to any horse for very long."

She reached for her bridle and undid the throat latch and noseband, then slipped the reins over Trickster's head. Gently she slid her right hand under Trickster's jaw and onto her nose. With her hand positioned there she had better control, and Trick was fussy about taking a bit.

"Let's try to get off to a good start, okay, Trickster?" Jenna said gently.

Trickster refused to open her mouth. "You know, Foxy never does this," Jenna chided. She slipped her left thumb into the corner of Trickster's mouth. Reluctantly Trickster opened her mouth and took the bit.

"Nothing like the taste of human for breakfast, eh?" Jenna asked. "I'm glad you see who's boss. Just try to keep that thought when you decide to refuse a jump out there."

Trickster was without a doubt the best jumper Silver Creek owned. She had a reputation for unseating riders. Some people even claimed she *enjoyed* unseating them.

With her left hand under the pommel of the saddle

and her right hand under the panels at the back, Jenna lifted it up above Trickster's withers and placed the saddle. In some ways, getting to ride Trickster was quite an honor, she told herself as she reached under Trickster for the girth. She was an unpredictable horse, soft-mouthed and skittish, and it took a sensitive rider to anticipate her moods and handle her.

Still, it was Foxy Jenna had spent all year with. She was a tough, strong-willed, no-nonsense kind of horse. Riding her was like riding a bike. You just got on and rode. On second thought, maybe it was a little more like riding a Harley. A big, powerful, potentially dangerous kind of bike.

"Come on, Trick," Jenna said, leading her out of the stall. "Let's get this show on the road."

They walked out into the blinding morning sunlight. The other members of the class were already there. Seven riders. Melissa and Louisa Tisch were the only ones Jenna recognized.

"Trouble tacking up?" Claire asked sarcastically, looking up from her clipboard.

"We were having an intimate moment," Jenna said.

She looked over at Melissa and felt a twinge. She told herself it was the lumpy oatmeal she'd had for breakfast. But she had the annoying feeling it might have been something else. Like jealousy.

This was crazy. Everyone shared stable horses. She didn't own Foxy. Not any more than she'd ever owned Turbo.

Claire started them off with a walk and then an easy trot around the ring to get the horses warmed up. Jenna had the feeling she was in the company of more experienced riders than she'd been used to in her regular school-year class at Silver Creek. Not that they were probably any better than her. But at Silver Creek she'd always been the top, or one of the top, riders in her class. Here, she might well be just one of many.

Claire signaled them to stop. "I want to get a little better feel for your skills level," she said. "One at a time, I'd like to see each of you take a ride around the jump course. Just a quick check to see which skills we need to concentrate on first. Carolyn, why don't you start?"

Jenna watched a thin girl with a long brown ponytail make her way through the course on a beautiful gelding named Big Red. Smooth as silk, no problems. Impressive.

Maybe it was even possible some of these riders were better than Jenna. Her stomach seemed to be wandering around her insides, taking the grand tour. Weird. She never felt nervous when she was riding— except maybe at shows, and then it was mostly just the adrenaline rush.

Another rider, then another. All good, really good. Jenna thought of Katie, in her own class in another ring. Was this how she was feeling? This, well . . . nervous?

"Melissa?" Claire called.

Melissa took Foxy through her paces. On her third fence, a vertical, she left out a stride and took off from too far back, but for the most part, she kept a nice rhythm as she moved through the course. Still, Jenna thought Melissa seemed a bit timid. Foxy needed a strong rider, someone who wasn't afraid to take control.

"I think you're letting her drop a little," Jenna told Melissa as she and Foxy returned to the group. "Foxy's used to a little more contact with the reins."

"You need to give a horse a fair amount of leeway," Melissa responded. "Nothing turns them off jumping quicker than being pulled on the mouth."

"Jenna?" Claire called. "You want to teach class later? You're up."

Jenna urged Trickster into a collected canter. They took two turns around the ring, then approached the first fence. Jenna applied a lot of leg pressure, the way she usually did with Foxy. They cleared the first fence, but she landed hard, lurching forward and leaning on her hands. Jenna tried to recover and rushed Trickster into the next fence. It was a lousy jump, and an even lousier recovery. She continued around the course, but Trickster's canter was choppy, and no matter how hard she tried, Jenna couldn't seem to find her distance.

"I think maybe you're too aggressive with her," Melissa said when Jenna returned to the group.

"I think maybe you're not aggressive enough with Foxy," Jenna replied.

"Well, just because that's the way you've always done it doesn't make it right."

"I know Foxy like she's my own," Jenna said, more heatedly than she'd intended.

"Ahem," Claire said. "I hate to interrupt the brawl in the back there, but I was hoping to get a little more work done."

"It's not my fault she thinks she's the world's greatest horsewoman," Jenna muttered.

"Jenna," Claire said in a voice that spoke volumes.

"I was just giving you a little constructive criticism," Melissa said.

"Melissa," Claire warned.

"I can't help it if she's a—" Melissa cut herself off.

"A what?" Jenna demanded. Trickster shifted nervously beneath her.

"Why is it I suddenly feel like a kindergarten teacher?" Claire asked the others.

"I want to know what she thinks I am!" Jenna cried.

"Okay, that does it. Time out. You two ride out to some neutral corner and fight this out," Claire said. "And don't come back till you've resolved it. Or one of you is mortally wounded."

"But why should I be penalized?" Melissa demanded. "She's the one with the mouth—"

"I know, Lord love her," Claire said sympathetically. She waved. "Tootles."

"Claire—" Jenna began.

"May the best woman win," Claire said.

With a great heaving sigh, Jenna led Trickster out of the ring toward the muck heap. "I am not too aggressive with Trickster," she said as she brought her to an abrupt halt.

"Yes, you are," Melissa replied. "But let's face it, that's not what this is about."

Jenna frowned. "Oh, really?"

"You've been picking on me since the moment I got here," Melissa said, running her fingers through Foxy's silky mane. "I tried to give you the benefit of the doubt, but I want to put you on notice right now." Her voice took on a sharp edge. "We're going to be sharing the same tent for weeks, and I'm not going to put up with your racist crap—"

"My *what*?"

Melissa stared her down. "We both know that's what this is about."

Jenna felt her jaw drop. "Wait a minute. You actually think I don't like you because you're *black*?"

"It's called prejudice. Welcome to the real world."

"Whoa. Hold on a minute. You've got me all wrong."

"Oh, so you *do* like me? You have a funny way of showing it."

"No, no. I'm saying I *don't* like you. At all."

"I rest my case."

"But it's not because you're black. I mean, give me a break. It's because you're an obnoxious, pushy goody-goody who's too perfect for her own good."

"I believe you mean it's because I'm an obnoxious, pushy goody-goody who's too perfect for her own good and happens to be *black*."

"Don't tell me what I think," Jenna shot back.

"I don't believe that's all there is to this."

"You're right. I also don't like you because you think you're a better rider than I am."

Melissa crossed her arms over her chest. "The truth hurts."

"And because you stole my horse."

"Now, *that* is not true, Jenna, and you know it."

Jenna didn't answer.

"How about the fact that *you're* obnoxious and pushy and think you're a better rider than *I* am?" Melissa demanded.

"You forgot too perfect for my own good."

"Trust me," Melissa said, "I didn't forget. And I didn't steal your horse."

Jenna sighed. "I know," she admitted irritably. "It just sort of feels like you did."

Seconds ticked by. "So what you're saying," Melissa finally said, "is that you hate me because of who I am, not what I am?"

"Well, duh."

"This is great." Melissa cracked a smile. "I'm so relieved you hate me."

"I sincerely hope no one's listening to this conversation," Jenna said.

"Me, too."

"So now what?" Jenna asked.

"I guess we should go back and make the happy announcement that we can't stand each other."

Jenna smiled. "You know," she said, "you may be good at jumping, but I'll bet you're not as tough as I am in a flat-out race."

"We can't race," Melissa said. "Claire would be so upset."

"She's already upset. In my case, she sort of expects to be."

"You seem to bring that out in people."

"Over there, just as far as that big pine." Jenna pointed to a flat field past the main paddock where she'd raced many times before.

"I don't know—"

"Just one little race. Come on. You are so anal."

Melissa laughed. "Thanks. I hate you, too." Without another word, she took off in a wild gallop, leaving Jenna in her dusty wake.

"I *knew* I didn't like that girl," Jenna muttered, and then she raced off in hot pursuit.

"How was class?" Jenna asked Katie when she and Melissa returned to the stable after they'd cooled down their horses.

Katie was in Say-So's stall, where she had him cross-tied so she could clean his right hoof with a pick. "Okay, I guess. We did a lot of exercises. Margaret had us stand in the stirrups at a trot and ride without reins while we posted. I really missed you, Jen."

"I missed you, too," Jenna said. "There wasn't anyone to laugh at my stupid jokes."

"I laughed at your general stupidity," Melissa pointed out.

"We sort of got expelled," Jenna explained. "And then we went through the back meadow and raced."

"I won," Melissa said.

"She cheated," Jenna countered.

Katie gently set down Say-So's leg and moved to the other side. She lifted his leg and carefully began to scrape out stones and bits of mud with her hoof pick, working from the heel toward the toe. "I'm glad to see you two are speaking, at least."

"We have an understanding," Melissa said, soothing Say-So with a gentle ear scratch.

"We understand we can't stand each other," Jenna said.

Katie looked up. They were both grinning. She was afraid to ask what they were talking about.

"Did you hear about the pony picnic tonight?" Katie asked.

"What's that?" Melissa asked.

"See what you miss when you cut class?" Katie teased. "We're having a picnic dinner down by the lake tonight with all the horses. They even get a picnic, too."

"Sounds like fun," Melissa said.

"Sharon said she'd rather have a cavity filled. Without any painkiller."

"How did Sharon do in class?" Jenna asked.

Katie shook her head, but it was too late. Sharon poked her head out of Escape Route's stall halfway down the aisle. "Sharon sucked," she said loudly. "It took her most of the class just to get in the saddle."

"Sharon, that's not true," Katie said quickly. "You did great on those exercises. Better than I did."

"Like I said, I sucked."

Katie rolled her eyes. She'd spent all morning trying to connect with Sharon, and all she'd gotten for her trouble was sarcasm or silence.

"Just ignore her," Jenna whispered.

Sharon stepped out of the stall. "Well, I'm off to enjoy a nutritious, wholesome lunch. I don't know about you, but I'm hoping they microwave up some of last night's leftover taco masterpiece."

"Wait," Katie said. "We can all eat together. I just have to finish here—"

"No rush," Sharon said. "I'll go on ahead so you can talk about me."

"Jen," Katie said when she was sure Sharon was out of earshot, "I've been meaning to tell you something. We found out what happened to Sharon. Claire told us. Sharon was on her horse when they got hit by a drunk driver. Her horse was killed, and Sharon was in rehab for months."

"Oh, man." Jenna leaned against the wall.

"Which explains why she wouldn't talk about Cassidy," Melissa said. "I feel like such a jerk, bringing her up."

"How could you have known?" Katie said reassuringly as she set down Say-So's leg. "Anyway," she continued, "Claire said she's kind of having a hard time getting through to Sharon, and I thought we should all try not to give up on her, even if she is kind of, well—" She paused. Jenna's face was pale. Her eyes glistened. "Jen?" she said. "You okay?"

"There you are!" Claire came marching down the aisle. "Jenna, there's a call for you in the office."

Jenna wiped a hand across her eyes. "I'll meet you guys at the lodge."

"After you dine," Claire said, "I have a little token of my esteem for you and Melissa. The last four stalls on the end need mucking out, and I think you're just the women for the job." She smiled sweetly. "And the next time you skip class to play Kentucky Derby, you can muck out the entire stable."

"Sorry," Melissa said with a sheepish grin.

Claire marched off. "By the way," she called over her shoulder, "who won?"

"I did," Melissa replied.

Katie watched as Jenna followed Claire out of the stable. "Is she okay?" Melissa whispered. "She didn't even point out that I cheated."

"I guess the story about Sharon got to her."

"Jenna, having a sensitive moment?" Melissa asked. "She's probably just pouting because she lost our race."

Katie smiled, but as she watched Jenna disappear out the stable door, she had a feeling something else was bothering her, something that had nothing to do with losing a race.

9

"Line two," Margaret called from Rose's office. "You can take it in here, unless you want some privacy."

Jenna stepped into the tiny room that served as the nerve center of Silver Creek Stables. Margaret was putting away manila folders in an old oak filing cabinet.

"I hear you played hooky yesterday morning," she said, shaking her finger at Jenna.

"Guilty."

"Next time, let me know when you race. I'll take bets."

Jenna sat at Rose's desk. As usual, the cramped office was barely controlled chaos. Her desk overflowed with camp applications, horse magazines, and little pieces of scrap paper with notes Rose had written to herself. Propped on top of a somewhat dirty fish tank was a tray containing the remains of this morning's breakfast. A TV and VCR in one corner of the room were piled high with tapes of Silver Creek students. Trophies and ribbons lined the walls, along with Rose's antique horseshoe collection. Rusty, mud-caked, cracked—Rose didn't care, as long as the horseshoe was old. Jenna understood. Her entire ceiling at home was plastered with horse posters.

Jenna picked up the receiver. "Hello?"

"JJ, it's me! Legs! Your sister!"

Jenna smiled. "Yeah, that name rings a bell."

"I miss you tons and it's so boring and I gave Furball a bubble bath—"

"Whoa. Hold on. You gave the cat a bubble bath?"

"That's not why I called."

"When does summer school start?"

"Soon, I can't remember. They have a new bus with red on it. Are you having fun?"

"Kind of."

"Mom and I drove by Turbo's house yesterday and you know what? I think he looked sad."

Jenna paused. "I miss you, Legs," she said softly.

"I have a present for you. Well, it's sort of Mom's present, too. Listen."

"Listen to what?" Jenna asked, but it was too late. Allegra was already rattling around the room.

"Hi, hon." Jenna's mom got on the phone.

"Mom? How come you're not at the restaurant?"

"Allegra's new sitter canceled on me. She's going to come in for the dinner shift and help out, aren't you, sweetheart? How's camp? Do you miss us at all yet?"

"It's barely been a week, Mom. Don't push your luck."

"Hey, I'm a mom. It's my job to push my luck." In the background, Allegra was complaining. "Oops, I forgot. Allegra's got a surprise."

There was another rustle, then the sound of buttons being pushed. Through the receiver came the tinny sound of the TV. The voice of Barney came through, singing his trademark song.

Jenna groaned. She and Legs shared a personal hatred for Barney.

Allegra got back on the phone. "Did you hear? We taped *Barney* for you. Yesterday he did being jealous and it was so grommit."

Jenna laughed. *Grommit,* a combination of *gross* and *vomit,* was their made-up name for anything that made them want to throw up. Despite their mom's best efforts, they both agreed that tofu was grommit. Anything containing broccoli also qualified.

Jenna ran her finger along one of Rose's dusty horseshoes. She glanced over her shoulder at Margaret. "So what did Barney say about jealousy?" she asked quietly.

"I guess that it's bad. I'm kind of not sure. He was giggling too much."

"I gotta go, Legs," Jenna said.

"JJ? Are you sad about Turbo still?"

"No, Legs. He'll find a good home."

"JJ? I miss you."

"I miss you more. Say bye to Mom."

"JJ? I miss you really *lots.*"

"Bye, Legs."

Jenna hung up the phone. She stared at Rose's murky fish tank, lost in thought.

"Allegra a big Barney fan?" Margaret asked.

"She hates him. The guy can't stop giggling. Personally, I think he's on something."

"You know, you're awfully good with your little sister."

Jenna shoved back her chair. "I gotta go. I'd hate to miss those leftover tacos."

"Don't worry. They'll be there tomorrow. It's the miracle of reproduction. Every morning, the cooks open the walk-in and find dozens of new baby tacos."

Jenna left the office. Off in the distance, the noise of laughter and clattering utensils filled the lodge. But she wasn't hungry. Instead, she turned off toward the paddock, where several of the horses were frolicking. Foxy and Trickster were engaging in a game of horse tag. Big Red was dashing in circles, bucking like a crazy seesaw. Wishful Thinking, the black mare who'd been Claire's mount when she was younger, was busy rolling exuberantly in a patch of mud.

Jenna climbed up on the fence. It seemed like years had passed since she'd sat on a fence just like this, saying good-bye to Turbo.

In a way, she and Sharon were going through the same thing. Jenna tried to imagine what it must have been like, losing her horse in such a tragic way. Sharon must feel so angry at that driver. How could you contain that much anger? Wouldn't you just explode?

Of course, Jenna didn't have anyone to get angry at, not really. It was like her dad had said. Sometimes things just happened. That was all. You took your lumps and got on with life. There was no one to blame. Nobody.

Jenna caught herself humming the same tired Barney lyrics. She shook her head to clear them away, but it was like trying to wash out a permanent stain.

In the paddock, Foxy kicked up her heels. That was the nice thing about horses. Everything was so simple for them. Give them food, room to run, and some horse buddies, and they were content.

Being a human was a lot more complicated.

Sharon's journal
Day 15
I don't know why I'm writing in this thing. Because there's nothing but reruns on TV? Because I'm too tired to read? The only entertainment around here is the woman in the next bed who likes to show people the scar from her gallstone operation. She's worried it's infected. I've seen it four times already. In my medical opinion, it's fine.

Maybe that's why they let a bunch of us loose yesterday. Me. Courtney, the girl who's paralyzed from the waist down. Randall, the guy with bone cancer. Mr. Ruiz. (I'm not sure what's wrong with him. I guess he had some kind of stroke. He can only smile with one side of his mouth.)

They took us into this arboretum place, sort of a garden in the middle of the hospital. It was really hot for fall, Indian summer, so I'm guessing that was the idea—get the handicapped some fresh air, get some color in those pale cheeks. Or maybe the nurses just wanted to get rid of us for a few minutes. I can't really blame them. Yesterday I threw lime Jell-O at this nurse when I buzzed her for half an hour and she wouldn't bring me a bedpan. I know it was rude. But it was rude to make me lie there like that, wasn't it? She would have been a lot sorrier if I hadn't buzzed her.

So anyway, they wheel us down, the gimp gang, in our wheelchairs. We sit there on the patio, and I have to admit the sun kind of melts into me and the leaves are doing their quick-change number, red and gold and streaked, and after a while I'm feeling pretty good. So good I talk the gang into a game of poker (I just happen to have some cards in my robe pocket.) We don't have any money so we use maple leaves for chips.

And for a while I actually forget about That Day. It's easy not to think about it, surrounded by a bunch of other people who've been screwed by life, too. It's like some thief came in and ripped us all off, and maybe he took more money from some of us than from others, but hey, we all know how it feels so it doesn't really matter who has the most change left. You get so you don't even notice that Randall has this stump for a leg. Or that Courtney has to pee in a bag.

We're having a pretty good time (I'm winning practically every hand) and after a while Mr. Ruiz of all people says out of the corner of his mouth, "Hey, let's play strip poker." Of course we all think that's pretty funny, the idea of all of us with our messed-up bodies playing strip poker in the hospital garden, wouldn't that freak out the candy stripers, and then all of a sudden I hear them. C.J. and Kara and Justin and Natalie. And Alec, of course. They're at the edge of the garden. Kara has these big shiny balloons and Alec is carrying this single pink rose.

I'd avoided them as long as I could. I'd made my mom tell them I wasn't strong enough for visitors, but I knew it couldn't last forever.

I turn around, and they stop laughing and talking and just stare at me, at all of us, like we're some endangered species in a park zoo. After a second or two they run over and say hi and Alec gives me this sort of embarrassed kiss like it's our first date or something. And I intro the gimp gang and there's this long awkward silence. Kara says she's really sorry about Cass, what a horrible waste, and then she and C.J. start bawling, and I really think I'm going to lose it.

It wasn't the bawling that got to me. I expected the tears and poor-Sharon stuff. It was that look, when they first saw me, that look that said I wasn't part of them anymore. It's like when someone gets held back a grade. You swear you're going to stay friends, but of course you don't because you're a seventh grader and she's a sixth grader and she'll never know what you're talking about when you rag on the sub in geometry and there's this invisible wall between you that neither of you wants to admit exists.

I tell myself, *hey, it took me a while to get used to Randall.* I mean, it's hard not to look at a guy without a leg and think, *what is wrong with this picture?* Maybe with time, they'll treat me the same.

But I have this feeling that even if I could wake up tomorrow and walk out the hospital door like nothing had happened, they would still look at me differently. No matter what, they'll always be thinking, *I'm so glad I'm not her.*

Sharon closed her journal. Escape Route stood next to her blanket, munching on the dessert snacks she'd brought for him—apples, carrots, and rutabaga slices, cut lengthwise so he wouldn't choke if he swallowed them whole. The horses had already been fed and watered, and now it was time for everyone else. The cooks had packed fried chicken dinners in little baskets with red and white checked napkins.

Here at the far, narrower end of Silver Lake, the thin sandy beach quickly gave way to a grassy field. Fifty yards out was a tiny islet, just a few trees and a bird or two. It was shallow enough to wade to—or, if you didn't want to get wet, you could just about make it there by leaping from big rock to rock. Several people had tried already. Most had ended up soaking wet.

It was the kind of stunt Sharon no longer dared to try. It would put too much pressure on her weak leg, and besides, her brace wasn't really supposed to get wet.

Not that she cared. She liked sitting out here in the early evening light, the sun stretching out long copper arms as if it were trying to hang on to the edge of the world. She wasn't exactly a nature freak, not like Katie seemed to be. Sharon was more the mall-crawl type— give her a Gap and an Orange Julius any day of the week.

Still, she had to admit there was something to be said for this nature stuff. She'd never really paid much attention to it, not even when she and Cassidy were doing one of their frequent trail rides or meadow gallops. When Sharon was riding, she thought about riding. The truth was, she used to get annoyed at Cass when she just wanted to munch a dandelion or stare down a butterfly. Sharon could never wait to get in high gear again.

"I brought you a present."

Sharon looked up in surprise. It was Jenna, carrying a napkin full of something.

"Well, actually, it's for 'Cape." She passed the napkin to Sharon, then sat cross-legged on the edge of her blanket. "Sugar cubes and apples. Trickster's getting a potbelly. I'm putting her on a diet."

"Well, it's not like Escape Route couldn't use a tummy tuck himself, but what the hey. Here, 'Cape." Sharon held up a sugar cube and he wolfed it down, chomping noisily. "Lousy table manners. He says thanks."

Jenna fingered the edge of the blanket. She seemed to be struggling for words.

"What's going on over there?" Sharon asked, not because she cared but because she couldn't stand the awkward silence.

"Rose is putting together teams for an egg and spoon race."

"Egg and spoon? Is that an Olympic event?"

"In one hand you carry an egg in a spoon, and with the other hand you lead your horse."

"Hard-boiled?"

"Egg, yes. Horse, no."

"I don't think I'm up to the challenge."

"Good call. You want to come sit with us and take bets on who mushes first?"

Sharon looked out at the lake, ribboned with red and gold. "Correct me if I'm wrong, but are you attempting to be my buddy?"

"You know what Daniel-without-the-*le* said. We're supposed to be bonding."

"I'm not really bonding material, Jenna. I'm more the troubled outsider type. Sullen, brooding, potentially well armed."

Jenna leaned back on her elbows. She did not seem to be taking the hint. After a while she grabbed one of Escape Route's sugar cubes and popped it in her mouth. "Dessert," she explained.

"What year did you say you were, Jenna?"

"I'll be starting seventh."

"Well, maybe they do things differently in seventh, but in eighth grade, we call what I just dropped a *hint*. A big one."

Jenna grinned. "Yeah, I'm pretty slow on the uptake."

"What would work? *I want to be alone*? *Get lost*? A blow to the head with a blunt object?"

"Keep going."

Sharon sighed. "Look, I'm sure you're a very nice person, but I doubt we have a whole lot in common, so—"

"We do, though."

"Mutual dislike?"

"No, that would be Melissa and me." Jenna rolled onto her side. Her eyes were darkly serious. "I know about your horse."

"How?" Sharon demanded angrily. "Who told you?"

"Claire told Katie and Melissa, and they told me."

Sharon sighed. She should have known Claire wouldn't be able to keep her mouth shut. Well, they were bound to find out eventually.

"And anyway," Jenna continued, "I just wanted you to know . . ."

Here it comes, Sharon thought, *the I-know-just-how-you-must-have-felt speech.*

"See, I know it's not the same thing, exactly, but I just lost my horse."

"You mean it died?"

"No, Turbo's still alive, but it sort of feels like he died." Jenna paused. "I mean, I had all these big plans for him, and then bam, suddenly they're all gone."

"But he's still alive."

"Well, yes—"

"And you're still walking."

"Yeah, but—"

"Then I don't see how you could possibly know how I feel."

Jenna sat up. She looked as if she might be on the verge of tears. "I'm not saying I went through anything that bad, Sharon. I just meant I know what it's like to have something you love just all of a sudden disappear, okay?" Her voice caught. "And I know . . . I mean, I can *imagine* how mad you must feel."

"I'm not mad. The driver served his time in juvenile detention. He felt terrible. My being mad wouldn't change anything."

"You didn't resent—"

"I did. But I'm done with that."

Jenna bit her lower lip. "I guess I just thought you might want to talk to someone."

"Look, Jenna, just because I ended up in your tent, I'm not your very own personal burden."

"No. You're Daniel-without-the-le's very own personal burden," Jenna tried to joke.

Sharon took a deep breath. She didn't want to sound so mean. She just wanted to be left alone. Was that so hard to understand?

"I know you guys mean well," she said softly. "It's just that I get so tired of always feeling like someone's rehab project. I just came here to ride, that's all. Just ride."

Jenna thought for a moment, then stood. "I'm sorry about what I said," she muttered. "Turbo isn't like Cassidy. I didn't mean to compare or anything." Her hands flopped at her sides. "I guess I didn't mean anything."

Sharon watched her departing back. She could see Melissa and Katie waiting expectantly on their blanket. Jenna shook her head.

It wasn't the same. Jenna couldn't possibly understand. She couldn't know what Courtney or Randall or Mr. Ruiz had gone through. She couldn't understand Sharon. People like them didn't need the help of people like Jenna. With help came pity.

10

"I'm telling you, he's hot for you, Katie."

"He is not hot, and would you please spit out your toothpaste? You look like a rabid dog."

"So did Jake." Jenna spit out her toothpaste in a graceful arc. It landed two sinks down in front of Melissa. "Two points!" Jenna cried.

Melissa curled her lip. "That was truly disgusting."

Jenna took a little bow. "What can I say? You can't hide natural talent. And speaking of natural talent, that Jake guy has a bright future in pro egg-spoon circuit. Although I'm pretty sure he tried to trip the guy who came in second."

"He did not," Katie said as she rinsed her toothbrush.

"See?" Jenna said. "She's defending him already. I'm telling you, it's true love." Jenna stuck her fingers down her throat and made convincing gagging noises.

"I think they'd make a cute couple," Melissa said. "Although he is an older man."

"He gave her his winning egg, you know," Jenna said. "Doesn't that mean they're going steady?"

"Could be they're engaged to be engaged," Melissa said as she rubbed Noxzema on her face. "I mean, an egg's better than jewelry. You can't fry up an ID bracelet."

"It's the gift that keeps on giving."

Katie tugged a comb through her hair. "He didn't even say anything to me, you two. He just tossed me the egg and smiled. So could we please drop this?"

"Drop?" Jenna shook her head. "Not a good idea, Katie." She nudged Melissa. "It's in her sweater pocket, you know."

"It is not," Katie lied.

"What are you going to do when it rots?" Melissa asked as she dried off her face.

"I think you're both jealous," Katie said, jutting her chin.

"I have a boyfriend," Melissa said. "Even if he is a zillion miles away."

Jenna rolled her eyes. "I'm holding out for a guy with more class. The kind of guy who'll give me eggs *and* bacon. Maybe even toast."

Someone flushed a toilet, eliciting a scream of protest from the showers. "You're supposed to yell *flushing*," Katie called. "The water temperature gets really hot every time someone flushes."

"I feel like we're really roughing it," Melissa said. "My last camp I had a private bath."

"I like this better." Jenna gathered up her toothbrush and toothpaste. "It has that familiar school-locker-room charm."

They headed out into the cool night. The girls' and boys' bathrooms were located in small cement buildings on opposite sides of the main lodge. Katie glanced casually over at the other side as they left.

"Looking for the egghead?" Jenna teased.

"I was just taking in the view."

"She was looking, all right," Melissa confirmed.

"Actually, I was looking, but not where you think." Katie pointed toward one of the training rings, lit by a garish light attached to the stable. Claire was in the center of the ring, trying to work with Luna on a lunge line. Luna alternately bucked and balked, refusing to acknowledge Claire at all.

"Poor Claire," Melissa said. "She's got her work cut out for her."

They took the path toward their tent. Pine branches laced together to form a dark canopy overhead. "You're not going to turn into one of those guy-obsessed bimbos who are always checking their blush in the girls' room, are you?" Jenna asked.

"I don't wear blush," Katie pointed out. "I have a natural supply."

As they neared their tent, they could see Sharon through the mesh window flap. She was lying on her cot, reading a small blue fabric-covered book.

Katie paused. "Anyone got a new brainstorm on Sharon?" she whispered.

"I told you," Jenna said. "She doesn't want to be friends."

"Maybe it was the way you approached her," Katie said. "You can be kind of blunt."

"You can be *really* blunt," Melissa added.

"Maybe I was." Jenna leaned back against the trunk of a big oak. "I guess I was trying to tell her that I understood how she must be feeling because I'd sort of lost a horse, too. But as soon as I opened my mouth

I felt like a jerk because it isn't really the same thing at all. I mean, at least Turbo's okay."

She stared up at the trees. White veins of moonlight streaked her face. "I was trying to explain that I understand how you want somebody to be really angry at—" She stopped herself. "Never mind. You guys are right. I should never try to handle the sensitive friend stuff."

Katie put her arm around Jenna. "You're great at the sensitive friend stuff."

"I always put my foot in my mouth. Remember when your parents split up and the first thing I asked was who was getting custody of your tarantula?"

"Yeah, but afterward you bought me a double Wretched Excess."

Melissa frowned. "A wretched *what*?"

"It's this great chocolate fudge dessert my dad makes for the restaurant," Jenna explained. "Part cake, part ice cream. It'll cure anything."

"I thought it was a health-food restaurant," Melissa said.

"It is, when my mom's in the kitchen. When my dad's cooking, watch out. They have a running argument about the menu."

"Wretched Excess, huh? I'll have to remember that," Melissa said. "There've been a few times since my mom and dad broke up when I could have used one."

"I'll have Dad whip you up one sometime," Jenna said. "If you play your cards right." Jenna glanced over at the tent and sighed. "Well, anyway, I guess I should probably just keep my distance from Sharon for a while."

"She'll like you much better that way," Melissa joked.

Jenna elbowed her in the ribs.

"It's simple reverse psychology, Jenna," Melissa said. "You know, where you say or do one thing, knowing it will have the opposite effect?"

"Reverse psychology," Katie repeated. "Hmmm." She snapped her fingers. "That's it. Melissa, you're brilliant!"

"I am?"

"She is?" Jenna asked.

"I think I have a plan for Operation Sharon," Katie exclaimed. She reached over to give Melissa a hug.

Something crunched. Katie stepped back. She slipped her hand into her sweater pocket and retrieved a handful of yellow ooze.

"Does this mean you and Jake are breaking up?" Jenna asked.

"That was fun today, wasn't it?" Katie called to Sharon as they walked their horses around the ring to cool them down.

"What?" Sharon looked over her shoulder. "I don't remember having any fun."

They headed out the gate toward the stable. "The pole work," Katie said. "I never thought walking and trotting over ground poles could be exciting, but it's such a good way to practice your jump position. I like to imagine I'll actually be jumping over real fences soon."

"I didn't used to have to pretend," Sharon muttered. "I wish Margaret would let me move into one of the more advanced classes."

Katie started to respond that Sharon didn't seem ready for that, but she knew there was no point in arguing. Just then, she noticed Claire heading toward the nearby training ring. She was leading Luna, who was resisting her every step of the way, yo-yoing back and forth on the lunge line like a frustrated toddler.

Okay, Katie told herself. *Time for Operation Sharon.*

"Poor Claire," Katie said. "She's got a handful there. There must be so much involved in breaking a horse."

Sharon stopped Escape Route and took a sidelong glance. "Yeah. It's a lot of work."

Katie eased up alongside 'Cape. "Don't feel bad about what Claire said," she whispered.

Sharon was eyeing the filly with the same dissecting look of a show judge. Katie waited hopefully. Was she going to take the bait?

"What'd you say?" Sharon asked absently.

She was no good at being conniving. Jenna. Now, *Jenna* was conniving.

"I *said* don't feel bad about what Claire said. You know, about you not being up to it."

Sharon snapped her head around. "Up to what?"

"Nothing. Really, nothing." Katie slapped her palm to her forehead. "Jeez, I'm such a jerk. I mean, you'd expect Jenna to open her big mouth, but usually I'm a little more tactful."

She nudged Say and started toward the stable. Sharon followed her. "Look, it's too late now. If you don't tell me what Claire said, I'll go ask her myself. And I'll tell her you're the one who spilled it."

Katie stopped again. "Sharon, don't take this the wrong way. She was just thinking about your . . ." She nodded at Sharon's braces. "You know. She said she was just as glad you weren't interested in helping train Luna, and that she shouldn't have put you on the spot by asking, because you obviously aren't—"

"Aren't what? Up to the big challenge? Is that it?"

Katie looked away. "She didn't mean it like that, Sharon."

Sharon's mouth was a thin line. "Thanks, Katie."

"For what? Blabbing?"

"No. For telling me the truth for a change. It's nice to see at least someone thinks I can take it."

As Sharon trotted off, Katie felt a stab of guilt. She hoped she was doing the right thing. If her little maneuver backfired, she was really going to feel lousy.

She turned Say-So around and headed back to the training ring.

"Claire?" Katie hooked her index finger. "Come here. I have a confession to make."

"This isn't like an I-chewed-gum-during-class confession, is it? Because I prefer my confessions juicier than that."

"It involves manipulation and deceit."

"Now we're talking." Claire eased Luna over to the rail. Say-So tried to say hello, but Luna wasn't having any part of him.

"But it's for a good cause."

"That's what they all say."

Katie leaned forward and whispered, "I told Sharon you didn't think she was up to helping you train Luna."

"But I want her to help! I'm dying for her to help. Not that she's remotely interested, of course, since she thinks it's just a consolation prize—" Claire stopped in mid-sentence. "Duh. I just got it." She raised her brows. "Not bad, not bad at all, Katie Freud. A little child psychology, eh?"

"She seemed pretty PO'ed. I'm not sure if it did any good or not."

"Katie, my dear. I'm impressed. This sounds like something Jenna might have done. It was sneaky, it was underhanded, and it required overacting."

"I know. I can't wait to tell her. She'll be so proud."

Katie rode off, Claire's words still ringing in her ears. She was right. This *was* the kind of scheme Jenna would have cooked up. Katie was used to that arrangement—Jenna, the leader, Katie, the follower. They'd always been inseparable. But maybe it didn't always have to be that way. She was getting along by herself in her class, wasn't she? She'd befriended Melissa on her own, too, without Jenna—although, fortunately for the tent, it looked like Jenna and Melissa were starting to get along better.

She kind of liked this new, improved Katie. Of course, before she got too carried away, she'd have to see if Operation Sharon really worked.

11

"Before we get going on our first overnight, a few rules of the road," Claire said to the assembled riders the next morning. "Some of this is old hat, so bear with me, those of you who've heard it all before."

Sharon gazed around her. All of the intermediate and advanced riders were going on this overnight. The beginners were taking a day trip to Silver Creek. Escape Route shifted beneath her, his ears pricked, his whole body on alert. Like all the horses, he was raring to go.

She was probably the only one there who would rather have stayed in her tent. This kind of ride could really take a lot out of you. You rode for longer periods of time on difficult and varied terrain, and that meant a lot of wear and tear on your muscles. No big deal for the others. A definite big deal for Sharon.

"First off, remember to watch out for low branches," Claire continued. "Your horse will take care of himself, but then, he's shorter than you are. When we get to water, and we will be crossing some shallow spots in Silver Creek, remember to give your horse plenty of

119

encouragement. Most don't mind it. Some, like Wishful Thinking here, even like it.

"Now, we're also going to be doing some hill work. When going uphill, be sure to lean forward and keep your weight out of the saddle. You want to free your horse up to use his hindquarters. On downhill stretches, keep vertical and don't zigzag down. Keep a contact on your horse's mouth, but let him use his head and his neck. He'll need it for balance so you can both descend safely." Claire paused, tapping her finger on her chin. "Okay, okay. I can see I'm boring you all. We'll cover more as we go along. Everybody got their bedroll and backpacks?"

The group responded with a murmur.

"Everybody got their horse?"

Laughter this time.

"For those of you who are keeping score, we're going to head around the edge of Silver Lake, through the state park trails to—oh, never mind. You'll see soon enough. Let's hit the road!"

They took off at a leisurely trot. Sharon sat it to conserve her leg muscles. Posting still put more of a strain on her legs and weak ankles than she would have liked. She tried to relax, but her muscles, tight knots of nervous energy, were already rebelling.

They'd taught her how to meditate in rehab for times like this. It was supposed to help keep your muscles from cramping up. You took deep breaths from the diaphragm and concentrated on nothing but your breathing. No thoughts, nothing but you and your breath. If you did happen to have a stray thought, you were supposed to imagine it was a balloon, floating away on the breeze.

Sharon let her abdomen rise and fall with deep cleansing breaths. She closed her eyes and tried not to think. It didn't work. She was thinking about Claire, about what Katie had revealed yesterday.

Sharon's not up to it. Where did Claire get off, deciding what Sharon was up to? Claire, who'd shoved her into a nursery-school–level riding class. Claire, who didn't think Sharon had the stamina to handle a bratty filly.

She breathed again. She imagined Claire in a big red helium balloon. She felt better, watching her float off into the stratosphere. *Good-bye, Claire. Be sure to send a postcard.*

She opened her eyes. There was Claire, leading the group on Wishful Thinking, her curly dark hair bouncing in the breeze. She was not, much to Sharon's dismay, floating away in a balloon.

They reached a long open stretch of sandy beach hugging the gentle waters of Silver Lake. *Enjoy this,* Sharon commanded herself. *It's beautiful. Relax, enjoy the scenery, enjoy the feel of Escape Route.* She closed her eyes and imagined the sun melting the hard knot in her left calf like an ice cube.

Claire held up her hand. "Everybody feel like a canter?"

Her suggestion was met with cheers of approval. *Good,* Sharon thought, opening her eyes. A canter would be easier on her. She could relax into the nice, rocking, one-two-three beat and maybe work some different muscles.

Unfortunately, Escape Route had a much rougher canter than Cassidy. Either that, or Sharon had a much weaker seat. She found herself tensing, unable to relax and let her hips absorb the motion. She should have felt like she was on a rocking horse. Instead, she might as well have been riding one of those mechanical bucking broncs.

Her left foot slipped out of the stirrup. How humiliating. She was riding like a complete novice. It took three tries before she could regain her footing.

Melissa rode up on her right. "Sharon?" she asked. "You okay?"

"Fine."

"I could ask Claire to slow—"

"Excuse me, Melissa. Maybe I'm mistaken here, but I was under the impression *I* was the one who won the championship at the Classic," Sharon said as she struggled to maintain her balance. "Was that some kind of clerical error?"

Melissa shrugged and dropped back.

Sharon lost her stirrup again, her right one this time. While she worked to retrieve it, she kept herself busy, imagining Melissa in a big green balloon, floating into the sky with Claire.

Melissa squirmed in her sleeping bag. Maybe she wasn't cut out for this outdoorsy stuff. She kept hearing things in the woods. Probably big things, with big teeth and big appetites.

She reached into her backpack and pulled out a pen and a notepad. She'd almost brought her laptop, until Jenna had told her she was missing the whole point of roughing it.

The campfire sputtered, sending tiny orange fireworks flying. Everyone was asleep, their sleeping bags arranged around the fire like spokes in a giant wheel. Only Sharon stirred occasionally, shifting in her sleeping bag and moaning softly. Melissa wondered if she was in any pain. She'd been even more tight-lipped and grim than usual, all through dinner and the late-night horror stories around the campfire.

Melissa clicked her pen and began to write.

Dear Aisha and Chelsea,

Greetings from Silver Creek Riding Camp, which is not turning out to be quite the disaster I'd been afraid it would be. Actually, I should say greetings from the middle of Silver Creek State Park. We're on an overnight.

Hard to believe, I know—yours truly in the wilderness. But it's really been fun—cantering along a beach, making our way up a windy mountain trail, cooking weenies over the fire . . . watching them drop into the flames and turn to charcoal . . . toasting marshmallows . . . watching them drop into the flames and turn to charcoal. Can you tell I'm starving?

It's night now, and everyone's asleep but me. Our horses are in this paddock nearby. The night's full of noises. Not city noises, like we're used to. Nature noises. Weasels and bears and things. I kind of like it. I think.

I even kind of like my new tentmates. I mean, nobody could replace you guys, but I can see how Katie and Jenna and maybe even Sharon and I could get to be friends—

Melissa heard a noise, a sort of startled grunt. She tossed down her pen and stared at the vast dark woods.

"Relax, it's just me," Sharon whispered.

"I thought you were a weasel. Were you dreaming or something?"

"Yeah, dreaming." Sharon sat up on her elbows. Her face was pale and shadowed. "What's the notebook for?"

"I'm writing a letter. To my friends. I guess I should say my former friends."

Sharon rubbed her eyes. "I thought maybe it was a . . . you know, a diary."

Melissa nodded at the blue fabric-covered book jutting out from Sharon's backpack. "Is that what that is? A diary?"

"That?" Sharon's expression tightened. "That, Melissa, is the past."

"The past." Melissa savored the word. "Sometimes I wish I could go back there."

"You can't go back to who you were," Sharon said, looking up at the sky. "A girl told me that once."

"Do you think she was right?"

Sharon sighed. "For her, maybe. Not for me." She rolled onto her side, away from Melissa.

Melissa sat silently. The noise of the woods swelled and shrank, like a single living, breathing thing.

"Sharon?" she whispered. "You asleep?"

"Not anymore."

"I just wanted to say that I'm sorry about today. You know, on the beach? I didn't mean to upset you. I mean, you're the best rider I've ever competed against."

Sharon rolled onto her back. Something in her face had changed. Her eyes glowed like the crumbling fire. "Remember the jump-off at the Classic?" she whispered.

"Unfortunately, yes."

"What a rush."

Melissa smiled. "I still get fired when I think about that last triple."

Sharon's eyes darkened. "It was a tough course."

"Anyway, I just wanted you to know, in my book, you're the best."

"I'm sorry I blew up. It's just . . ." Sharon closed her eyes and took a deep breath. "It's just hard, being set apart, having people treat you differently. You can't imagine what it's like."

"I can imagine," Melissa replied.

Sharon opened her eyes. She looked at Melissa and nodded thoughtfully. "Yeah," she said at last, "I suppose you can."

The next morning they threaded their way back down a different route, a thin winding mountain trail. Dewy ferns tickled the horses' feet as they picked their way through the rocky path, slowly descending. On their right was a steep incline where gnarled, stunted pines clung. On their left, towering trees, mostly oaks and pine, provided shade from the already intense morning sun.

They descended slowly, single file, taking in the sounds. The steady clop of hoofs. The annoyed screech of a jay. The secret rustles in the trees, wood creatures spying on these big, strange animals with their even stranger loads.

Katie kept herself busy trying to sit tall in the saddle without leaning while giving Say-So enough rein as he made his way down. Thinking about her position took her mind off the steep incline to the right.

Every so often she'd turn around in the saddle to check on Sharon, who was following behind her. She looked tired and drawn, but Katie was afraid to ask how she was doing.

As they rounded a bend, Katie scanned the woods, hoping to catch sight of a rabbit or a deer. A flash of something caught her eye on the path just ahead. Her heart knew what it was before her head did, and she felt a tight clench of fear. A big black snake was slithering across the path.

Say-So saw it, too. He reared up, front legs flailing wildly, and let out a piercing scream of fear. Katie managed to hold on for a split second, until Say-So stumbled back on a thick tree root.

The impact sent Katie tumbling backward into the air. The world whirled, green, blue, brown, a terrifying kaleidoscope, and then she landed with a hard grunt on the very edge of the path.

"Katie!" someone cried.

Sharon. Katie recognized her voice, and then she was slipping down the rocky incline, inch by precious inch.

12

"Take my hand."

Katie was hanging on to a gnarled tree root jutting out at the edge of the incline. Fifteen feet below her, sharp, tumbled rocks waited for her.

"Come on, Katie," Sharon urged. "You can't hang on forever."

All around them, people were yelling, jumping from their horses, running to the rescue. But all Katie seemed able to do was stare into Sharon's eyes. Her pupils were huge, dark holes of fear.

Sharon took Katie's hands in both of hers. She was on her knees, and the awkward position sent hot streaks of pain up her legs. She leaned back and pulled with all her might.

One good yank with Sharon's strong arms, and Katie belly-flopped back onto the path.

Spread-eagled on the ground, Katie looked at Sharon gratefully. "My hero," she said.

Sharon laughed as she pulled a twig from Katie's jumbled hair. The others swirled around them, a blur of concerned noises.

Claire and Rose were the first there. Claire had a coil of rope around her shoulder. "Great," she muttered. "I was all set to play Rescue 911 and you beat me to it, Sharon."

Rose knelt down next to Katie. "Any cracked bones? Sprains? Bruises? Broken nails?"

Katie sat up, moving her arms and legs gingerly. "Well, my ego may need major surgery," she joked, but her eyes were filled with tears.

Jenna and Melissa ran over breathlessly. "It's not enough you have to fall off, you have to fly off the side of a mountain?" Jenna demanded. She brushed dirt off of Katie's jeans. "You okay?" she asked softly.

Katie managed a nod.

"Hey, I can top flying off a mountain," Melissa said. "I once got thrown off into a giant pile of pig dung."

"That's nothing." Jake appeared on the edge of the crowd. "I once got thrown at a show while I was warming up."

"That's happened to everybody at least once," Rose assured him.

"Not directly into the lap of a judge," Jake pointed out. "A judge with a vanilla milk shake in one hand and a double cheeseburger in the other." Everyone laughed, even Katie. "Of course, she said my form was impeccable, under the circumstances."

"Is Say-So okay?" Katie asked.

"Margaret's checking him. He may have sprained a tendon. The same leg he bruised last year getting into a trailer."

"The snake's fine, though," Claire added.

Katie looked back at Say-So, her eyes filled with

worry. Her hands were trembling.

"Claire," Sharon said, "maybe you should give us all a little break."

"Good idea. Let's take ten minutes to enjoy the sights and munch some granola, gang."

Katie's whole body was beginning to shake. Sharon knew the feeling. She'd done the same thing when they'd told her about Cass. It was part shock, part pain, part realizing the magnitude of what you'd just gone through.

"Katie?" Melissa asked. "You want to go sit with us on that rock over there?"

Katie didn't answer.

"Maybe you should give us a minute or two," Sharon said.

Jenna frowned. She looked at Melissa, who gave a little nod. "Okay," Jenna said, sounding reluctant. She touched Katie on her shoulder. "We'll be right over there if you want company."

Katie leaned forward, knees bent, her face buried in her arms, and silently sobbed.

Sharon hesitated. She didn't really know Katie. Jenna did. Even Melissa knew her better. And Sharon wasn't exactly the touchy-feely kind of friend you turned to in times of trouble. She should have kept her mouth shut.

"I'm sorry," Katie managed in a choked whisper. "I'm such a wimp."

Awkwardly, like someone holding an infant for the first time, Sharon put her arm around Katie's shoulders. "It's scary. I know. All of a sudden you realize how vulnerable you are."

Katie looked up, sniffling. "Is that how . . . you felt?"

Sharon nodded. Katie wasn't trembling quite as much. Good. Maybe she wasn't totally screwing this up.

"Everybody falls, Katie," she said. "Haven't you heard that old saying? They say you have to fall off your horse seven times before you're a true rider."

"I have fallen before," Katie said. "But it was always in the ring. Here, outside, you realize how much can go wrong. To you. Or to your horse—" She stopped herself. "Oh, Sharon," she whispered. "I wasn't even thinking about Cassidy. I'm sorry."

"Don't be. It's true."

Katie took a shuddery breath. Sharon felt another stab of pain in her leg. She'd dismounted so hard she'd probably bruised it. But she didn't want to move, not quite yet. Not till Katie was ready.

"Maybe I'm not . . . Maybe I'm not cut out for this," Katie said. "I'll never be a great rider, not like Jenna or Melissa or you."

"Me?" Sharon laughed shortly. "Me? The only one in class who still finds mounting a challenge?"

"It's different for you. For one thing, at least you know what it's like to be a great rider. I mean, you've been there. And for another, there's a good reason you can't do some things. Me, I have no excuse."

"You know," Sharon said, "when I was in the hospital, we had this perky occupational therapy woman. Toni, that was her name. She kept coming around with her little cart, trying to convince us to draw or paint or make little clay animals. I told her, 'Look, I can't draw a straight line, I'm no artist,' but she wouldn't leave me alone. So finally I took this glop of clay from her one afternoon."

Sharon paused. She was babbling on about something Katie couldn't possibly relate to. Maybe she should quit while she was behind.

"Go on," Katie urged, sniffling again. "What happened to the glop?"

Sharon sighed. "Well, I don't know. I guess I started playing around with it. And everything I made looked just like Gumby, kind of like some protoplasm you'd look at under a microscope. But it was kind of fun. Well, not fun, like a good gallop, but sort of distracting. After a while I started making horses." She rubbed her leg.

"And you got better and better and eventually they turned out beautifully, right?"

"No, they looked like protoplasm, too. You see what I'm getting at?"

"No."

"I'm not very good at this, am I?" Sharon smiled ruefully. "I'm trying to say that even though I wasn't any good at sculpting, I liked it and that was enough. Why do you ride, anyway?"

"At first, because Jenna talked me into it. She was always going on and on about the speed and the exhilaration when she'd take a jump, and I thought, why not?"

"And is that why you keep riding?"

"Well, come to think of it, no. I'm not even ready to jump." Katie rubbed the dirt off her boots. "Sometimes I feel like there's something wrong with me because the reason I love to ride is, well, just so I can be near such incredible animals. Is that crazy?"

"Sounds pretty sane to me, as long as you're having fun."

Katie nodded. "I am. I mean, I was, up until a couple minutes ago."

"You don't have to be a gold medalist to have fun riding, Katie. I may never make anything more than Gumby horses my whole life, but do you think that will keep me from sculpting?"

"You mean you're still working with clay?"

"No way." Sharon shrugged. "What am I going to do with a bunch of horses who look like the victims of some horrible radiation accident?"

Claire approached, shaking her head. "Bad news, Katie, my girl. Say-So's out of commission. You'll have to double up."

"She can ride with me," Sharon said.

"You sure?" Claire asked.

"I can handle more than you think, Claire," Sharon said, unable to keep the resentment from her voice.

Claire and Katie exchanged a look. "Okay, then."

Katie stood unsteadily. She brushed off her knees, then reached out a hand to help Sharon up.

"What a pair," Sharon said. She walked over to Escape Route and stroked his neck. "Lucky you, 'Cape. You get two for the price of one." She sighed. "I should warn you, Katie, you won't be pairing with the most coordinated rider on the planet."

"Hey, like you said, it doesn't matter," Katie said, smiling. "As long as it's fun."

For a moment, hearing her own words repeated back to her, Sharon almost believed them.

Sharon's journal
Day 103
Big date today. Randall, the guy from the hospital

with the bone cancer, calls me up, says grab your crutches, girl. You and Courtney and me are going to a basketball game. I'm thinking, yeah, right, but after about a half an hour of whining he talks me into it. It's not like I've been doing a lot of socializing, so I figure it will get my mom off my case.

It's only the first time we've gotten together since we'd all "graduated" from the hospital. His mom drives us in her van to this big old gym in a middle school, deserted since it's a Saturday afternoon. I swear it takes us an hour to pile out of that van. I've got my big old braces and my crutches. Courtney has her motorized wheelchair she calls her "Mercedes." And Randall has his new leg, which he calls, for some reason that escapes me, "Jerome." I guess I should name my braces something. "Ugly" and "Uglier," how about that?

We get to the gym and there's a bunch of guys there, just an afternoon pickup game, and they're bouncing around sweating and swearing and just generally being guys. Most are high school age, older by a couple years than Randall. He high-fives some of them and I whisper something to Courtney about how they're not exactly the Knicks, but Randall overhears me.

"Hang in there," he tells me. "They've got this one guy who'll knock your socks off." Which Courtney points out would be difficult, what with my industrial-strength orthopedic shoes.

We sit on the sidelines and Courtney and I are kind of looking at each other like, *if we wanted to go on a bad date, Randall, we could have come up with plenty of other options.*

Then all of a sudden Randall dives into the game and starts dancing around that court like Shaquille O'Neal. Okay, like Michael Jordan on a very bad day. But still and all, it was incredible, that magic leg of his. He blocked, he faked, he dribbled, he made so many baskets we lost track.

After a while Randall comes jogging over, all sweaty, and says, "So?"

"So," I say, straight-faced, "your hook shot sucks." And then I reach over and Randall and Courtney I are hugging like crazy, sweat and all.

Then Randall tells us he's a much better basketball player than he used to be. Courtney and I look at each other like, *yeah, right, Randall.* But he swears he's improved. He says he used to barrel right through people when he was charging for a basket. Now he's wilier, he waits, he uses his brain more. He sees an opening and takes it.

"Please," Courtney says. "You're telling us you're glad this all happened?"

"Give me a break. I'm not a fool." He laughs. "I'm just saying I'm a different basketball player, that's all. It's . . . well, kind of interesting."

Randall claims there's one other benefit from losing his leg. Thanks to his stay in the hospital with us, he's a much better poker player.

I could still take him for every penny he has, however.

Sharon closed her journal and looked up at Luna. For the past hour, she'd been sitting in the filly's stall reading, the same way she used to do her homework in Cassidy's stall.

Luna eyed her suspiciously. She wasn't at all sure she liked this human interloper. Still, Sharon hadn't moved or startled her. She'd just sat very still, to show she wasn't a threat, humming to herself now and then.

Sharon stood awkwardly, grabbing the automatic waterer in the corner of the stall for support. Her leg still hurt from this morning's "rescue mission," as Katie had taken to calling it.

Sharon tucked her journal inside her jacket for safekeeping. She wondered what had ever happened to old Randall and Courtney. They'd sort of lost touch since her move.

She'd never understood how Randall had made the transition from two legs to one so effortlessly. Maybe it hadn't been so effortless. Maybe he'd just put on a good show.

Courtney seemed to have adjusted pretty well, too, all things considered. In her last letter, she'd told Sharon she'd gone to a college dance in her wheelchair, where she'd managed to "dance" every dance.

Was it really as easy as they made it seem? Or were they just able to settle for less than Sharon was?

Sharon took a step closer to Luna. "Want to play school?"

Luna pawed the ground and snorted. "I know, you sweet old girl," Sharon said gently, letting Luna get used to her voice. "You've had some lousy teachers, but hey, it happens. Mrs. MacLachlan, my third-grade teacher, caught me eating paste in art and to teach me a lesson, she made me eat the whole jar."

Luna flicked an ear at Sharon. "Pretty dumb, huh? The only thing she taught me was the value of a stapler. But not all teachers are such idiots. Me, for example. I helped my uncle break lots of horses while I was growing up." She held out her hand. Luna sniffed, then tossed her head. "I hate that word, *break*. This is about putting things together, not taking them apart."

Sharon closed the stall door and went to the neatly arranged tack room, where she gathered up the equipment she would need. First she got the lunge line and the lunge whip. The long leather-handled whip, with its rawhide lash, was for reinforcing the directions she'd be giving to Luna. Hanging on the wall she found a lunging cavesson, a training halter with rings on a reinforced, padded noseband.

As she returned to Luna's stall, she checked her watch. Everyone was out in the far meadow playing musical tires, which involved placing several old tires in a circle, then playing a sort of musical chairs on horseback. She probably could count on a good half hour with Luna alone. Plenty, since she'd undoubtedly run out of patience long before that.

"Come on, sweetie," she whispered, running her hand over Luna's neck and shoulder. "Let's go get ourselves some education."

But Luna wasn't interested in higher learning. It took four tries and several minutes of soothing before she'd allow Sharon to slip on the halter.

At last Sharon clipped the lunge line to the cavesson. "Well, we're off to a great start," she muttered as she eased Luna out of the stable.

She glanced up at the twilight sky. A pale slice

of moon peeked over the trees. So that's where Luna had gotten her name. Her light dapple gray coat did remind Sharon of the moon. You could almost make out the man-in-the-moon on her hide.

"How come it's a man-in-the-moon anyway?" Sharon asked, keeping her voice low and soothing. "Why not woman-in-the-moon?"

Luna eyed the ring nervously. She obviously didn't like this closed-in place with its post-and-rail fence and soft sand-covered ground. This was the kind of place where these strange two-legged animals demanded that she do uncomfortable, unfamiliar things. And when she didn't understand, this was the place where they got angry at her.

Sharon led Luna into the ring. Instantly the filly tensed even more. She danced restlessly, tail swishing wildly, ears flicking, and eyed the rail apprehensively, as if she were planning her escape route.

It was not a good sign. It was much harder to untrain a horse than to train one. Sometimes bad training could never be entirely undone. Horses had very long memories.

"Poor Luna," Sharon said soothingly. "Who scared you so badly, pretty girl?"

She let the lunge line out about six feet, keeping the remaining coil in her right hand. With the whip in her left hand extended toward Luna's hindquarters, Sharon had formed a rough triangle, with herself at the apex.

"Walk," Sharon said, giving Luna a gentle tap with the whip while pulling on the lunge line.

Luna yanked back on the line, snorting contemptuously.

Sharon tried again. Again Luna balked. This time she almost seemed to be enjoying it.

"We seem to be having a difference of opinion," Sharon said.

She shortened her line slightly to get even more control. "Walk," she commanded again. Her uncle had taught her to use sharp, precise commands, each with a different inflection to make it easier for the horse to recognize vocal instructions. *Trot* was short and sweet; *come* was softer, gentler.

More taps and pulls, and at last Luna began a reluctant, jerky walk.

"That's the way," Sharon said in a voice filled with praise. "Here we go, girl."

Luna pulled against the line, aiming for the rail. Sharon tapped and jerked back.

"See, we're aiming for a circle here," she explained. "This would be a line. A circle is, well . . . not a line. Got it?"

They came to a standoff near the fence, when Luna decided the lesson was over.

"Excuse me, but did I say *whoa*?" Sharon asked. She reached down to rub her aching leg. "If, for example, I'd said *whoa*, then this would be a major breakthrough. But unless my memory fails me, *whoa* is not the operative word here. *Walk* is."

Luna blinked at her. Her disdainful expression reminded Sharon of a naughty preschooler—which was, come to think of it, exactly what she was.

Sharon leaned again the fence. "Time out." She was tired. Not that she'd admit it to anyone, but the overnight had worn her out. And Luna wasn't exactly helping matters.

Sharon just didn't have the temperament for this. Her uncle had often told her that when she was jump training with Cass. He said she pushed too hard, too fast. She asked too much. And she got annoyed too quickly. "A horse is like a wild child," he liked to say. "You've got to be patient to outsmart it."

The truth was, he'd always done the serious work on training. She'd been there for the fun stuff, but she hadn't had the perseverance to fight it out, day after day.

Sharon sighed. What she really wanted to do was yell at Luna, yell at the top of the lungs that this was for her own good, why couldn't she see that?

This is for your own good, Sharon. She heard the voice of Claire at the PET center. Was this how Claire and her other therapists had felt with Sharon? This frustrated?

"Look, Luna-tic, not all people are bad. You've got to trust some of us. Even if you got hurt once along the way," Sharon said. "I know it's hard. Man, do I know it's hard."

Luna swished her tail in annoyance.

"Yeah, well, I can kind of see your point," Sharon said.

After a few more halfhearted tries, Sharon led Luna out of the ring. It was getting dark, anyway, and the rest of the gang would be back soon. At least no one had seen her flop miserably. She'd had enough public embarrassment to last a lifetime.

This was a dumb idea. She wasn't trainer material. She didn't have the persistence or the subtle touch. Claire had been right. Sharon wasn't up to this.

Too bad, too. Poor old Luna deserved better.

13

"Knock, knock! Tent inspection!"

Margaret and Daniel stepped into Thoroughbred Tent. It was afternoon, and the girls were sprawled on their cots. Sharon was reading, Katie was drawing on her sketch pad, and Melissa was loading her camera with fresh film. Jenna was dozing, snoring slightly.

"Welcome to our humble home," Sharon said. "Do you count off for rats?"

"That wasn't a rat, Sharon," Melissa scolded. "That was a roach with an attitude."

"Speaking of attitudes," Daniel said curtly, "do you really think it was necessary to put shaving cream on all the toilet seats in the ladies' room the other night?"

"We were celebrating our victory in the musical tires competition," Melissa explained. "It sort of got out of hand."

Jenna opened an eye. "Some of that was whipped cream."

"Well, you didn't have to write *Thoroughbrats Rule!* on the shower wall," Daniel insisted. "That was very ungracious."

"Besides, you blew your cover," Margaret added, trying to hide a smile.

"Sounds like I missed something," Sharon said.

"We didn't think you'd want to . . ." Katie began.

"Oh, you should always let me know when you're defacing public property."

"Do you see?" Daniel asked Margaret. She started to sit on the edge of Jenna's cot, then noticed a black banana peel and thought better of it. "Do you see what I'm up against?" She pointed a bright red fingernail at Melissa. "And you, Melissa! I at least thought I could count on you for some leadership. You're as bad as the rest of them."

Jenna nodded. "We corrupted her, it's true. So how are we doing on the tent inspection, Margaret? Flying colors, right?"

"That depends. What's that pile in the middle of the floor?"

"Underwear, socks, candy bar wrappers, you name it. It's our recycling pile. We're very environmentally conscious."

"You're recycling your dirty clothes?"

"It was that or wash them," Sharon pointed out.

"We're still cleaning up from the overnight," Katie added.

"That was two days ago," Daniel reminded her.

"Hey, how's Say-So doing?" Katie asked. "Didn't Gary check him out again this afternoon?"

"He said it's definitely a sprain. Not too serious, but he'll be out of commission for a few weeks."

Katie's face fell. "I feel like it's my fault," she said. "If I'd had better control of him, he might not have hurt himself."

"It wasn't your fault," Sharon said. "It could have happened to anyone."

"And that leg was already weak," Margaret added. She chewed on the end of her pencil, surveying the tent. "All right. I'll only take off two points for general cleanliness. But I'll give you one point back for ecological awareness."

"Way to go, gang," Jenna cried.

"Not way to go," Daniel corrected. "You're now dead last in the tent competition. You guys are ruining my counselor résumé."

"But we won the tires," Katie protested.

"We had to disqualify you for unsportsmanlike use of hygiene products," Margaret explained.

Two figures appeared in the tent doorway. "Can we come in?"

"Mom!" Jenna cried. "Legs!"

Allegra climbed onto Jenna's cot and grabbed her around the neck. "Canter!" she commanded, her light brown curls bouncing. She waved at Katie. "Hey, Katie!"

"Hi, Legs. Are you our new tentmate?"

"I wish," Allegra said.

"Everybody," Jenna said, "this is Allegra, my sister and my mom. Mom, you know Margaret and Katie. That's Melissa and Sharon, and Daniel, our tent adviser."

"Without the *le*," Daniel added. "Nice to meet you, Ms. McCloud, Allegra. Jenna and her tentmates have certainly made an impression around here."

Jenna's mother cocked an eyebrow. "What is it you've done, Jenna?" She slapped her hand to her cheek. "Whoops, sorry. I was in mother mode there for a second. I forgot we're not supposed to be here at all. But Legs was a little worried about her new summer school class, and she misses you so much, hon. I thought maybe if she saw how much fun you're having at camp, she'd feel better about everything."

"It smells like poop in here," Allegra said.

"That would be goat poop," Sharon said as she climbed out of her cot. "I've got somewhere to go," she said vaguely. "Nice meeting you, Ms. McCloud. You, too, Allegra."

Allegra frowned at Sharon's braces. "Are you a horseback rider?"

Jenna felt herself tense up. Kids could be so blunt. Worse yet, so could Sharon.

"Legs—" Jenna cautioned, but Sharon just smiled calmly.

"Yes," she said. "I am."

Allegra nodded. "Cool. Me, too, someday."

"Come on, kid, let's you and me go talk," Jenna said quickly.

She headed out into the meadow, doing her best to gallop. "Know what?" she said when they reached the lake. "You weigh a ton."

Jenna eased Allegra down and they sat at the edge of the lake. The waves stained the sand with dark brown half-moons.

"So, what's the deal with school?" Jenna asked. "I know it's a new teacher. But it's the same school, only for summer."

"I'm not going." Allegra peeled off her shoes and socks and began to bury her feet.

"Man, that's too bad for Cory, huh?" Cory was

Allegra's best pal. "I think he was sort of counting on you."

Allegra kept burying.

"You know, Katie was scared to come to camp here. I had to promise her I was coming."

Allegra looked up. "Katie?"

"Yep."

"Katie wasn't afraid."

"Yes, she was." Jenna combed her fingers through Allegra's silky hair. "But now she's fine. What if Cory's afraid?"

"He's not." Allegra examined a smooth gray stone. "I don't think."

"Sometimes people don't say what they feel."

"You do."

Jenna hesitated. "Not always."

Allegra pursed her lips. Her face was tight with concentration. "If Cory was afraid, he'd be scared to go without me because I took advanced beginner swimming and he never even took water babies."

"Good point."

"And also lunch because I always let him eat my granola bar. Don't tell Mom."

"You wild woman, you."

Allegra considered. "If you weren't here, what would Katie be doing?"

"Probably watching *Barney* tapes all day. Just like Cory, if you don't go."

Allegra sighed. "I have to go, then. For Cory."

Jenna gave her a hug. "Tell him it's all right to be afraid sometimes, okay?"

"Okay." Allegra unearthed her feet. "JJ, do you still love me?"

"Of course I do."

"You didn't maybe come here because you were mad at me?"

"Legs, why would I be mad at you?"

"I don't know." Allegra tossed her stone into the lake. "Stuff."

"Listen to me," Jenna said. "There's no stuff that could ever make me mad at you. Got it?"

"Got it." Allegra stood, brushing sand off her shorts. "Can I go see the horses now?"

Jenna nodded and Allegra took off. Jenna watched her run and felt a surge of love. She wished she could protect Allegra from the world. Everything was harder for her because she was disabled. Everything always would be. There was so much she didn't understand.

And yet, she thought as she tossed a stone far out into the gray-blue water, maybe she understood more than Jenna realized.

Jenna was in the Silver Creek driveway, waving good-bye to Allegra and her mom, when she heard footsteps behind her on the gravel. She turned to see Claire, Melissa and Katie approaching. All three sported broad smiles.

"Come on," Katie called. "We've got something to show you."

Jenna gave Allegra one last wave. "What's up?"

"Whatever you do, don't make a big deal out of this," Claire warned her.

"Big deal out of what?"

"Katie's devious little plan worked," Melissa said.

They turned the corner past the office and the training ring came into view. Sharon was in the ring with Luna, talking to her in a soothing voice.

"Score one for Katie," Claire whispered.

Just then, Sharon caught sight of them watching her. She let out some length on the lunge line and walked over to the fence. "Don't say it," she said.

"Say what?" Claire asked as they approached.

"Don't say you were right all along about me not being up for this."

"But—"

Katie held up her hand. "Sorry, Claire," she said. "I sort of blurted it out."

Impressive, Jenna thought. Katie showed great promise as an actress. Or maybe a politician.

Claire pretended to give Katie an annoyed look.

"The point is," Sharon said, "you were right. I can't handle it. I'm not getting anywhere with Luna. My uncle always told me I wasn't patient enough to be a trainer."

"Looks like you're doing better than I did," Claire said. "Is this your first time with her?"

Sharon looked at the ground. "No. We've had a few go-rounds. I don't know why I keep bothering. It's a waste of my time and hers."

"I guess if you can't handle it," Claire said, exchanging a look with Katie, "there's no point in wasting your time. And Luna's. I'll just tell my friend she's a lost cause."

Sharon grimaced. "We'll never be able to back her at this rate."

"Back her?" Katie repeated.

"Train her to accept a rider," Claire explained.

"She won't even walk on a lunge, you know," Sharon added with a frustrated sigh.

"I know. Believe me." Claire turned to go. "Well, go

ahead and put her back in her stall, Sharon. At least you gave it a try." She winked at the girls. "Let's go check the mail, gang. See if anybody got any good care packages from home. I'm holding out for some chocolate chip cookies."

"I'm going to hang here for a minute," Jenna said. "I already had my family togetherness for the day." She climbed on the fence. "You mind?"

"Suit yourself. I'm sure it's good for a laugh." Sharon leaned against the fence, eyeing Luna from a distance.

For a while neither spoke. "Cute kid, your sister," Sharon finally said.

"You have any brothers or sisters?"

"Sean. He's thirteen and thinks he's the next Joey Lawrence. And Kelly. She's nine."

"Allegra's eight." Jenna ran her hand along the rough edge of the fence. "She seems younger, I know, because she's—"

"She's adorable," Sharon interrupted. She pulled on her lunge line. "Come," she said.

Luna yanked back with all her might.

"Fine," Sharon muttered. "You win, you mule. You ass. You—" She ran out of steam. "Help me out here, Jenna. Can't you see I'm having a tantrum?"

"You flea-ridden bag of bones," Jenna offered.

"A cliché, but it'll do." Sharon shook her head. Damp red tendrils of hair stuck to her forehead. "Maybe it's not me," she mused. "Maybe it's Luna. We could send her to a special school for slow learners." As soon as the words were out of her mouth, she gasped. "Oh, that was brilliant."

"It's okay."

"No, it's not. I should know better. I don't know where my brain was, I was still thinking about Luna and it just rolled out—"

"Really. It happens all the time. People mean well, but it comes out wrong. You get used to it. Once my mom and Legs and I were at the grocery store and this lady said something about *she seems so bright, under the circumstances*, and for some reason I just lost it."

"Lost it how?"

"Lost it like I threw a banana at her butt. I unpeeled it first, of course. A nice, steady curve ball, actually, from all the way in dairy." Jenna sighed. "I got grounded for two months, but it was worth it. It gave new meaning to banana split."

Sharon looked pensive. "Lime Jell-O."

"What?"

"Lime Jell-O. That's what I used one time when I was mad over the same kind of thing."

"You can get more distance with a banana."

"Come," Sharon said again, and this time she managed to reel Luna in, inch by inch, like a giant fish, until she was close enough for them to stroke. Luna stood nervously, barely tolerating their affection, ready to bolt if they made a move she didn't like.

"Well, anyway," Sharon said, "I guess your sister might as well get used to it. It's like the world's divided into them and us. People will always look at her the way they look at me. Like they're thinking, *I'm so glad that's not me.*"

"Legs just stares right back," Jenna mused. "I think she can tell when people are being cruel, and when they're just uncomfortable. She always gives them the benefit of the doubt. It took me longer than her to figure out that sometimes people aren't being mean. They just plain put their foot in their mouth."

"You have to work to get your foot in," Sharon said.

"Look at you. You just did it about Allegra."

"That was just a slip, it wasn't—"

"You don't have to tell me. My foot has a permanent address in my mouth."

Sharon scratched Luna's ear. "You're not trying to bond with me again, are you?"

"Nothing personal, but you're not worth that much effort, Sharon."

Jenna climbed off the fence. She wanted to go somewhere, do something. Ever since Allegra's visit, she'd felt tired and hyper at the same time, like she wanted to take a nap on a galloping horse.

"You know," Sharon said suddenly, "Allegra's lucky she has you to run interference for her."

"No, she's not." Jenna clenched her fists. She hadn't intended the words to come out with such force.

Sharon looked up in alarm. "I just meant . . . now, don't go taking this wrong, too. I just meant she doesn't have to feel like a burden or something . . ." Her voice faded.

"But she *is* a burden," Jenna blurted. "She is! She's the reason I can't have Turbo; she's the reason my parents are always too preoccupied to notice if I even exist; she's the reason I always have to worry. I mean, when I'm baby-sitting, it's like twice the responsibility because you can't count on her. And when we go out, someone's always there to stare and make things difficult. Sometimes I just think if she weren't around how much easier—" She covered her mouth, horrified at the words spilling out like lava.

A look of recognition dawned on Sharon's face. "That's exactly how my brother and sister feel about me sometimes," she said. "Not that they'd ever admit it."

"God, Sharon," Jenna whispered, "I don't even know why I said those things. Don't listen to me, I guess I'm just upset about Turbo or something. I'm sure your family doesn't feel like that—"

"Of course they do," Sharon said quietly. "Sometimes. I mean, I would. They've had to give up things because of all my medical bills. And I'm always the center of attention—not that I want to be." She shrugged. "I just wish they'd get it out in the open. I know how they're feeling, but everybody tiptoes around it like there's this invisible pile of resentment in the middle of the house. The truth is, it's kind of refreshing to hear you come right out and say it out loud, if you know what I mean."

A wrenching sob made its way up Jenna's chest. She leaned against the fence, her head buried in her arm. "What kind of sister am I that I would feel like that? That I could get mad at Legs for something she can't control?"

"You're a perfectly normal sister."

Jenna looked up. "I'm total scum."

"Like I said, a perfectly normal sister." Sharon reached over and stroked Luna's mane. "Maybe you should tell Allegra how you feel."

"Why would I do that?" Jenna demanded, horrified.

"Because she probably knows it anyway."

Jenna thought for a minute. "How would you feel if your sister and brother told you something like that?"

"Relieved. Sort of like popping a zit."

"Nice comparison."

"I was trying to find something you could relate to."

Sharon started to lead Luna away. "Anyway, that's my advice, for what it's worth. Probably darn little."

"Sharon?" Jenna said. "Sorry I bawled. I try not to make a habit of it."

Sharon glanced over her shoulder. "Me either," she said. "Personally, I've never really seen the point."

14

"Jenna?" Rose rapped gently on the side of Jenna's head. "You in there somewhere, darling?"

Jenna looked up from the bridle she'd been cleaning. "Did you say something, Rose?"

"I said you just won the New York lottery and you're a multimillionaire ten times over."

Jenna rubbed her damp sponge on a glycerine bar. "Whatever."

Rose sat down on a storage chest near Jenna. "Is there anything you feel like talking about, kid? Something's obviously bugging you. Why else would you be in here all by yourself, cleaning tack without anyone even nagging you?"

"I was just thinking."

"Now I *know* there's something wrong." She reached for the bridle. "Might this be about a certain chestnut gelding?"

"Yes. Well, no. Well, yes and no." Jenna set down her sponge. "I guess it's more about me than about Turbo."

She looked over at the phone on the wall. It was strictly for emergencies in the stable, nothing else,

153

and everybody knew it. "Rose, do you think I could use the phone over there? Just for a minute."

Rose hesitated. "Promise you won't call Paris?"

"I won't even call New Jersey."

"Have at it." Rose passed her the bridle and strode to the doorway. "And about that horse. I'm sure he'll find a good home, hon. Things always have a way of working out."

Jenna dialed before she lost her nerve. Her mother answered. "Mom?"

"You miss us already. I feel so vindicated."

"Actually, I'm calling for Legs."

"We were just heading over to the restaurant and I'm already late. Your father's threatening to put double chocolate cheesecake on the menu instead of *tabouleh*. Keep it short and sweet, okay?"

A few seconds later Allegra got on the phone. "JJ? Guess what? Mommy heard that Turbo got—"

Allegra paused. Jenna could hear their mother talking in the background.

"Um, never mind."

"Tell me, Legs. It's okay. Turbo's not hurt, is he?" Jenna coiled the cord around her fingers nervously.

"No, he's fine. It's just . . ."

"Someone else bought him? Is that it?"

Allegra didn't answer. After some fumbling noise, their mother got on the phone. "Honey, I'm sorry," she said. "I was going to wait and tell you when you got home from camp. We stopped by K mart on the way home, and we saw Mrs. Shelby, and she said her husband thought he'd found a buyer for Turbo. That's all I know. I'm sure they'll take good care of him, honey—"

"It's okay, Mom." Jenna cleared her throat. "Would you put Legs back on?"

Allegra took the phone. "JJ? Are you mad?"

"Why would I be mad?"

" 'Cause I told. And 'cause you can't have Turbo 'cause of . . ." Her voice trailed off.

"Look, Legs. There's something I forgot to tell you."

"Uh-huh?"

"Remember by the lake, when you asked if I was mad and I said no?"

"Sort of."

"Well, the thing is, I was mad, for a little while. Because I really wanted Turbo, you know, and I had to be mad at somebody, even if it wasn't fair. And so, well . . . for a little while, I guess I was mad at you. Even though it was wrong. But I'm not, not anymore."

Jenna waited. She could hear the TV droning in the background. Suddenly she knew she'd made a terrible mistake. Why had she listened to Sharon? What did Sharon know about Allegra's feelings?

"Legs?" Jenna whispered.

"I got mad at Cory once," Allegra said thoughtfully. " 'Member when I lost my Pooh bear and I got mad at Cory only he didn't do it?"

"But Cory's still your best friend, right?" Jenna held her breath.

Allegra hesitated. "No."

"No?"

"Cory's my second best. Know who's my first?"

Jenna smiled. "Yeah, I think I know. I love you, Legs. Have fun at summer school."

Jenna hung up the phone. So Turbo had a new

owner. Well, no one could ever love him as much as Jenna would have. She waited for the pain to hit. She checked the tack room for things she could throw in anger without causing too much damage. Briefly, she even considered crying.

But all she could think of was Cory, Allegra's second-best friend.

"You know, Melissa," Sharon said as she stepped into the tent, "every time I see you it seems like you're writing another letter on that computer of yours."

"Every time I see you it seems like you're reading that little blue book of yours." Melissa looked up from her screen. "Don't you ever write your friends back in Vermont?"

"I'm not much for letters," Sharon said dismissively. "How'd it go with Luna?"

"You saw. It didn't go." Sharon flopped onto her cot. "Claire was right."

Melissa shrugged. "Too bad. She's a pretty filly."

"Pretty insane, anyway. Claire should never have taken her on."

"Hey, did you happen to overhear Claire and Rose at lunch?"

"I was pretty busy trying to decide between the tuna surprise and the taco casserole. Did I miss something?"

"They were right in front of us in line. I could have sworn they were talking about Jenna, but I couldn't make out what they were saying." She shrugged. "All I know is, lots of whispering was involved."

"Search me. I'm always the last to know."

Melissa went back to her computer, but after a few

more lines, she looked up. Sharon was staring at her intently. "Boy," Melissa said, "you must be bored if you're reduced to watching me type."

Sharon smiled apologetically. "Sorry. I was looking at that photo of you at the Classic, holding up your ribbon."

"Geeky picture, I know. I'm no Naomi Campbell."

"It's a great picture. You look so psyched."

"You must have lots of pictures of that day," Melissa said.

"I have this video, actually, my dad took. It's at the bottom of my duffel bag somewhere . . ." Sharon's voice faded. She seemed to be looking past Melissa to a place far away.

Melissa reached for the brass-framed photo. "I wasn't psyched, to tell you the truth. I know I didn't have a prayer, but I was really furious I didn't beat you. I'm what you'd call your basic sore loser."

Sharon grinned. "You're not the only one."

"My mom used to tell me if you put your mind to something, you can do anything, and I sort of took it to heart."

"I like that sentiment."

Melissa put down the photo and laughed ruefully. "So did I. That's why I tried to fly off the garage when I was six. I mean, I put my mind to flying, big time. I was going to fly to Kalamazoo."

"Why Kalamazoo?"

"I have no idea. I guess I just liked the sound of it."

Sharon laughed, a hearty, deep sound that surprised Melissa. She realized it was the first time she'd heard Sharon really laugh since she'd walked into the tent that first day.

"I'll tell you something, Melissa," Sharon said. "If you put your mind to it, you can be as good as I was—" she paused, "as I *am*. You've got the talent."

Melissa nodded. "Sure, I can ride. But what about flying to Kalamazoo?"

"There's only one way to fly, Melissa. Taking your horse over a jump."

Melissa heard her wistful sigh. "I don't know, Sharon," she said gently. "I like to think maybe there are lots of ways to fly."

"You can't always get what you want . . . You can't always get what you want . . ."

Jenna put her pillow over her head. If Silver Creek insisted on waking them up every morning with blaring music, did it have to be something from the Dark Ages? Please, her *mother* liked the Rolling Stones.

"You can't always get what you want . . . but sometimes you get what you need . . ."

Someone nudged her in the back.

"Beat it," she growled. "I was having this great dream. I was at the Preakness on Turbo, coming into the home stretch a length ahead."

No one answered. Strange. It was awfully quiet in the tent. She was generally the last to roll out of bed, although Sharon came in a close second.

Jenna felt herself slipping back into her dream. Something tickled her hand and she waved it off. Bugs. This tent was full of them. If you connected all the mosquito bites on her right leg, you'd have a map of Minnesota.

She heard noises, shiftings, rustlings. Jenna pulled her pillow off her head.

Quiet. Good thing. She had no desire to open her eyes just yet, not when she was about to cross the finish line.

Of course, her roommates weren't making it easy. Someone was messing with her hair. "Cut it out, Katie," Jenna said.

In response she got a big, wet nuzzle on her cheek.

Enough was enough. Jenna shot up. "Quit fooling around!" she screamed.

Big, melted-chocolate eyes blinked back at her.

They did not belong to Katie.

Jenna blinked, too. The tent was full of people—Rose, Claire, Gary, all her tentmates.

It was also full of horse.

"Turbo?" Jenna reached up to touch his muzzle. Then she touched the top of her hair, which was, as always, matted with snarls. She pinched herself, just to be on the safe side.

"Meet the newest addition to the Silver Creek stable."

It was Rose, grinning at the end of her cot.

"*You* bought him?" Jenna whispered.

"Ah, the mummy speaks!" Claire exclaimed.

Melissa smiled. "Too bad. I kind of liked her in shock."

"We needed a temporary replacement for Say-So, and we've been looking to add another horse." Rose shrugged. "Besides, he comes highly recommended."

Jenna leapt onto her cot and flung her arms around Turbo's neck. She looked over at Katie. "Did you know?"

"Not until yesterday evening when Rose clued us in. Believe me, it was hard to keep my mouth shut."

"*Our* mouths shut," Melissa amended.

Sharon stepped forward and ran her hand along Turbo's sleek neck. "He's beautiful, Jenna," she whispered. "You were right."

"Wait till you ride him," Jenna said.

"You mean you're actually going to share him?" Melissa teased.

Jenna stroked his mane while Turbo searched her cot for signs of food. "I don't even care that he's not mine. It's enough just to have him here."

"Thank Sharon for that," Rose said. "She's the one who put the idea into my head."

"Sharon?" Jenna repeated. "Thank—" She stopped. Sharon had vanished. "Where is she, anyway?"

"She just slipped out the door," Claire said.

"You can thank her later," Rose said. "Right now, I think you have more pressing concerns. That's one hungry horse, from the look of it."

Everyone departed, leaving Melissa, Katie, Jenna, and Turbo, who was busy sniffing out a box of Melissa's Cracker Jack. "Come on, guy," Jenna said, taking his reins. "Let's go have some real breakfast."

"You might want to get dressed first," Katie suggested. "Although I'm sure the guys would enjoy seeing you in your ratty T-shirt." She gave Jenna a long hug. "I'm so happy for you," she whispered. "And for Turbo, too."

"Katie?" Jenna whispered. "I'm not dreaming, am I?"

Katie swiveled Jenna's shoulders until she faced the mirror on Sharon's dresser. "You've got morning hair, Jenna," she pointed out. "And this tent was just filled with people. Why would you dream something that humiliating?"

As if to reassure her, Turbo nuzzled the top of Jenna's head.

15

"Hey, Luna," Sharon said as she opened her stall door. "It's me. The human you love to hate."

She checked the stable one last time for signs of Jenna, but it was lunchtime and the place was deserted. At the far end, Turbo's regal head poked out over his stall door as he got to know the new neighborhood.

She was glad for Jenna, but the girl was driving her crazy with her endless thank-yous. All she'd done was put the bug in Rose's ear, that was all. It was purely practical. Rose needed a horse, Turbo was available. If Sharon hadn't thought of it, someone else would have. But it didn't mean she needed to be Jenna's best friend for life.

She sat down next to Luna gently. For once, the filly was in a quiet mood. From her position on the hay, Sharon gazed at Luna's perfectly formed legs. It amazed her that an animal so powerful could look so fragile up close, like those blown-glass horses her grandmother displayed on a dusty shelf. You'd never believe that in the ring this delicate creature had the soul of the Terminator.

163

She wasn't quite sure why she'd taken to coming here, hiding out in Luna's stall. She told herself that she was letting Luna learn to trust her, but that was crazy. Hadn't she more or less given up on helping Claire train her? On the other hand, if she'd given up, why was she hanging out here like Luna's own personal horse nanny?

"You don't mind me coming here, do you, girl?" Sharon asked.

Luna flicked her ear, considering. Apparently she was willing to keep an open mind, as long as Sharon kept that infernal lunge line out of the picture.

Sharon opened her journal and sighed. She felt weary to her bones, and she didn't know why. Maybe reading back these scribbled pages was part of the problem. But she was nearly done with the journal now, and she couldn't seem to stop herself. It was like hiding out in Luna's stall. It just felt like the place she was supposed to be.

She thumbed through the pages until she came to an entry that caught her eye.

Sharon's journal
Day 171
Things I miss about Cassidy.

1. Watching her gallop through a meadow, airborne, pure energy. Pure freedom.

2. Visiting her in the paddock after school and leaning my cheek on her neck that's all hot from the sun.

3. Her horse smell.

4. Our tree game. We go through the woods, I find a low branch and grab it. Cass heads off, then jerks to a halt. She turns around and looks at me like *girl, you humans are some weird animals.* Then she shakes her head and gives me this snort of disgust and trots on back where I'm still dangling. I plop back onto her and we're off, Cass still carrying on about what a crazy person her owner is.

5. Muzzle nuzzling. Enough said.

6. Giving her her favorite treat—warm bran mash with some carrots and apples and a little molasses thrown in for good measure. Horse heaven!

7. A really great day, where every move we made together was perfect, and Cass knew how much I loved her.

8. A really bad day, where every move we made together was lousy, and Cass knew how much I loved her.

9. Her incredible ability to unlock every stall bolt ever devised.

10. Crying on her shoulder when I was sad. She always understood. Always.

11. The way she used to nicker when she saw me coming, then toss her head into the air and gallop over.

12. Braiding her mane and tail before a show. She was so vain, she loved it, and so did I!

13. Riding her, walk, trot, canter, gallop, jump, it doesn't matter, it was all perfect.

14. Sitting in her stall with her. Doing my homework, straw in my geography book, Cass nudging me to get it over with so we could go play.

15. Cass. Just Cass. There will never be another horse like her. Never.

It surprised Sharon, reading over that entry. She hadn't even mentioned the ribbons, the accolades, the skills. She'd just written about the fun of loving a horse. About the same things she'd been preaching to Katie after she'd fallen off Say-So.

She stood, moaning softly as she put weight on her sore legs. "No school today, Luna," she said quietly. "I think maybe you've been expelled."

Luna nuzzled her shoulder tentatively.

"Sorry, girl," Sharon said. "It's not your fault. It's me. Maybe we can still hang out together now and then, okay?"

She closed Luna's stall door behind her and walked down the aisle slowly, letting her stiff legs warm up. When she got to Turbo's stall, she stopped.

"You're one good-looking guy," she said, and he pranced over, nostrils flaring, tail up. He had a proud, showy way of moving. As if he were saying, *look at me, aren't I something?* Cass had been like that, too.

Turbo nudged her hand. She pulled it away. He had the strong hindquarters and hocks needed to power him over fences. Jenna had said Turbo had the makings of a great jumper. She'd been right.

Turbo tried another hand nuzzle, this time more insistently. *Let's play*, he was saying. *Let's play NOW*.

Sharon turned away. She was glad for Jenna, really glad. It surprised her, in fact. After all, she didn't even know Jenna very well.

Turbo let out a whinny that was half whine, half playful chiding. Sharon stopped in midstride, startled.

It could have been Cassidy's whinny.

She felt tears coming, but how could that be? She didn't cry. She didn't need to cry.

Suddenly Sharon was running toward the door, running from Luna and Cass and Turbo and a world where her days would always be counted from That Day. Her left brace caught on a wooden board. She stumbled, gathered herself up, and limped awkwardly into the sunshine.

But when she got outside, she stopped. What was she thinking? Where was she running? There was nowhere to go.

Wherever she went, no matter how far, That Day would always be there, waiting for her in her dreams.

This time, everyone was in the stands. The President, the mayor, Dr. A. Mrs. MacLachlan, Sharon's third-grade teacher, was there, holding a giant jar of paste. All the Silver Creek gang had shown up—Rose and Claire and Margaret and Gary, Jenna and Katie and Melissa, even Allegra. Courtney and Randall were there, too, although instead of his artificial leg, Randall was wearing a giant Slinky so he could bounce up to the basketball hoop without working up a sweat.

And for some reason, Turbo was there, sitting next

to Jenna. He was sitting in the stands, eating Cracker Jack while he read a *Sports Illustrated*.

The sun was a white ball. Sharon had on her lucky hair ribbon. She mounted Cassidy for the jump-off.

They were doing great, like they always did, walking away with it. The huge triple, the one that Cass hated, loomed ahead, but Sharon urged her on. *That's my baby*, she told her, *there you go*, and Cassidy soared fearlessly into the air.

This time, Sharon thought, *this time we'll make it*, but just as Cassidy was about to land, there it was— the beat-up sky-blue Ford. Sharon looked in vain for somewhere else to land, somewhere where she wouldn't have to look into the bleary, dangerous eyes of the driver, but everywhere she looked, there they were.

She gazed longingly at Jenna and Turbo in the stands. They were safe there. That's where she and Cassidy should be.

"There's something I have to tell you, Cass," she cried, and then the world grew cold and dark and there was nothing but the scent of hay and leather and blood—

"Sharon!" Someone was shaking her, hard.

Sharon opened her eyes. Katie. It was Katie.

She was in her tent, the smelly old tent at Silver Creek, and it was night. Moths bounced off the tent flaps. Melissa was holding her flashlight.

"You were screaming," Jenna said.

Sharon swallowed. "I must have been, to wake you," she tried to joke, but the dream was still holding on to her and this time it wouldn't let go.

Katie sat down on the edge of Sharon's cot.

"Sounded like a bad one," she said.

"Dreams don't mean anything," Sharon said quickly. "It's just your brain, letting off steam."

"Do you remember what it was?" Jenna asked as she tried to comb out a tangle of hair.

"I don't want to remember."

"Sometimes it helps," Melissa said.

Sharon sat up. The caring faces crowded her in like a fence. "Look, I'm sorry I woke you all. But it's no worse than the singing chipmunks Rose played yesterday on the loudspeaker, right?"

No one smiled. Their eyes glowed in the yellow blaze of the flashlight. They were watching her expectantly, just like they had in the dream, expecting something from her that she couldn't deliver.

"I don't want to remember," Sharon said again, but she knew that was all she'd been doing since coming here to Silver Creek. Remembering.

"If I'd had a horse like Cassidy, I'd dream about her, too," Melissa said. Her voice was soft, soft as the steady beating of the moths' wings.

"Not that dream," Sharon whispered. "Not like that."

"I wish I could have seen her," Katie said.

Jenna nodded. "I wish I could have ridden her."

"She was like Turbo, a little." Sharon looked at the Polaroid on Jenna's bureau, just a black square in the near-dark. "A real show-off, you know? And a flirt. You should have seen her jump."

"Sharon?" Melissa said gently. "What if we watched that video of yours?"

"I don't think I can."

"Come on." Jenna held out her hand. "Let's go watch it, Sharon."

"I don't want to remember," she said again.

"It'll be okay," Katie said. "We'll remember together."

16

"Where are we going to find a VCR at two in the morning?" Melissa whispered as they made their way down the dark path. Her flashlight carved a hole in the night.

"Knowing Jenna, she's planning to break into Circuit City and borrow one," Katie said.

"Funny you should mention breaking in," Jenna replied.

Sharon stopped. She wrapped her terry cloth robe around her and shivered. "Please, let's go back. This is crazy."

"Too late." Jenna held up Sharon's videocassette.

"I don't know why I gave you that," Sharon said. "What was I thinking?"

"Come on." Katie took Sharon's right arm and Melissa took her left. "It's too cold out here to argue."

They reached the complex of stable buildings. "So where's the VCR?" Katie whispered.

Jenna pointed. "Rose's office."

"No way," Katie whispered. "She'll expel us."

"No she won't. She'll kill us first. Then she'll expel us."

Jenna tiptoed toward the little white building next to the stable that housed Rose's office. A small storage shed for extra tack was attached at the back.

"I can't believe you, Jenna," Melissa said as Jenna tried the front door and two windows without success.

Katie and Melissa lurked behind her on the porch. "I told you she had more detentions than anyone I know," Katie said.

"That's not what I meant," Melissa said. "I meant I can't believe she's going to stage a break-in wearing bunny slippers."

Jenna stuck out her fuzzy brown feet. "These are not bunnies. They're moose. Meece. The big guys with antlers."

Sharon stood back from the others, shaking her head. "I'm going back," she said. Her voice was flat, but there was an edge of fear in it.

"No you're not. Not when we're risking life and limb and our standing in the tent competition for you."

"Good point," Melissa said. "Daniel is going to be so disappointed with us."

"Only if she catches us," Jenna said. "There's a window on the other side. I'm going to try it."

The others followed, watching as she fumbled with a shoulder-high window. "It's not locked," she reported. "Katie, come here."

"Why me?"

"Because you're the freakishly tall one."

"Take that back."

"Okay, because you're the statuesque model-like one."

"You'll need a leg up," Melissa said, joining them by the window. "I want you to know this goes against all my personal sense of right and wrong, Jenna."

"What are you saying? Don't do it?" Jenna asked as she removed her slippers and handed Katie the videocassette.

"No. I'm saying do it quickly."

"*I'm* saying don't do it," Sharon said.

Melissa cupped her hands and Jenna hoisted herself up onto Katie's shoulders. "Man, you're killing me," Katie complained. "It may be time to cut back on the tofu."

Jenna fumbled with the window. The glass rattled, echoing against the other buildings. "Hurry, will you?" Melissa urged. "Someone's going to hear you."

With a grunt Jenna managed to unstick the window. She hauled herself halfway in, her bare legs dangling in the air. Then, with one swift lurch, she launched herself inside.

She landed with a thud halfway down. Rose's desk.

Her foot was wet.

Correction. Rose's fish tank on Rose's desk.

Jenna removed her foot and shook it. She ran to the front door and unlocked it, motioning the others inside. "Hurry!"

Katie and Melissa tiptoed to the door, dragging Sharon along. Jenna carefully closed the door behind them.

"I can't see a thing," Katie complained.

"Don't turn on any lights," Jenna warned. "Follow me to Rose's office." They shuffled, one by one, into the small room. Jenna shut the door and pulled the curtains.

"It's wet on this chair," Melissa complained.

"I seemed to have landed in Rose's fish tank," Jenna explained. "Do you think a guppy really needs a tail?"

"You killed a guppy?" Katie cried.

"No, no," Jenna assured. "I think I just stunned him a little." She turned on a small desk lamp. "Now, take your seats, everybody."

In the garish light, all three of her friends looked pale, but no one looked paler than Sharon. Jenna suddenly wondered if she was doing the right thing. This had seemed like a great idea ten minutes ago. Now, she wasn't so sure.

She turned on the TV. Katie handed her the cassette. "Sharon?" Jenna asked softly. "Is this okay?"

Without a word, Sharon took the cassette from Jenna's hand and inserted it into the VCR. Then she sat down on the edge of her chair and stared at the screen, waiting.

The video flickered to life.

"That's the New England Classic," Melissa exclaimed. "Is this the year we were there together?"

Sharon nodded. The camera swayed and jerked. "Sorry about the camera," she said. "My dad's no Steven Spielberg."

The scene shifted to a group of waiting riders. "Hey," Melissa said. "That was my butt, I'm sure of it."

"It's a shame he didn't get a close-up," Jenna said.

Sharon waved to the camera. She was standing by Cassidy's trailer. Sean and Kelly and her mom crowded in, waving. Sean crossed his eyes.

"Cute," Katie said.

"You're already betrothed," Jenna reminded Katie.

The tape flickered and then suddenly Sharon was in the ring. It was an early round and Cassidy took the jumps like they weren't even there.

"Man, I wish I could do that," Melissa murmured.

Another flicker, a blank screen, and then it was the finals. Sharon watched anxiously, clasping and unclasping her hands. Her leg throbbed.

The camera panned. The stands were full of people she knew, friends and parents and fellow riders. The sun was a white ball. She was wearing her favorite lucky hair ribbon.

It was her nightmare, unfolding on a TV screen.

In the stands, people cheered. Cassidy took the course effortlessly, sheer grace, total control. They moved like a single animal. It was beautiful. It was perfect.

Ahead of them loomed the huge triple, the jump Cassidy hated. Sharon watched herself lean forward in the saddle in preparation. She was talking to Cass, urging her on.

"That's my baby," Sharon whispered the words as she watched.

Cassidy kept her stride. She trusted her, she knew it would be okay if Sharon said so.

Sharon froze, no breath, no thoughts, united with the picture on the screen, as Cassidy took off, soaring through the air like a hawk on the breeze. Pure freedom.

She closed her eyes. *This is where it all goes wrong,* she wanted to say, *this is where the truck comes and changes everything*, but when she opened her eyes Cassidy was floating to the ground in slow motion, as if she weren't quite sure she wanted to leave the air.

And in that instant when Cassidy touched the earth, Sharon felt something break free inside her and find its way to her heart.

She sobbed, a big, gasping sob, and buried her head in her hands.

Jenna turned off the tape and everyone gathered around Sharon, only this time she didn't feel trapped. She wanted them there. She wanted them to know Cassidy so they could remember her, too.

"Oh, God, I miss her so," she whispered, and then all she could do was cry some more.

After a while, she thought she heard something and she opened her eyes.

Sobbing. They were all crying, Jenna and Katie and Melissa.

"I'd give up everything to have her back," Sharon said. "I'd give up my legs if I could just have her back." She took a shuddery breath. "I thought I could just not feel it. I thought I could just go back to who I was and ride the way I did and I wouldn't have to feel it."

She wiped her eyes with the back of her hand. "Anybody got a Kleenex?"

Katie felt in her robe pocket. "Would you settle for a Mars bar wrapper?"

Sharon shook her head. She looked at her red-eyed, sniffling tentmates, searching for pity in their faces. But it wasn't pity she saw. It was something else. Something safe.

She stared at the blank TV screen. "Courtney was right. I'll never be that Sharon again," she whispered.

"And there'll never be another Cass. Ever."

"Who's Courtney?" Jenna asked.

"A friend, I guess." Sharon paused. "Like all of you."

17

"Thanks for dragging me here against my will," Sharon said as she stood shakily. "I feel better."

"Really?" Katie asked.

"No. Actually, I feel lousier than I have in a year and a half." Sharon forced a smile. "But it's a good kind of lousy. I think."

Jenna popped out the tape and handed it to Sharon. "Best movie I've seen all year."

"We really should be going, guys," Melissa said. "I hate to ruin the party, but this is, technically, a break-in, and they won't let me on the cheerleading squad with a prison record."

"Did you hear something?" Katie whispered. "I swear I heard something just now."

"Right, Katie," Jenna said as she headed over to Rose's desk. "I'm sure the FBI is hot on our trail."

"Come on, Jenna, what's holding up the works?" Melissa asked.

Jenna rubbed her sleeve across Rose's desk. "I'm trying to mop up the evidence," she said. She rolled up the sleeve and stuck her hand in the fish tank. "I have a feeling I knocked over this ceramic scuba diver. His head's buried in the—"

"Freeze!"

Two uniformed policemen leapt into the doorway, guns drawn. Rose and Claire, wearing robes and annoyed expressions, were standing behind them.

Jenna started to pull her arm out of the tank. "You heard them," Rose barked. "They said freeze. So freeze, already."

"You know these girls, ma'am?" a policeman asked.

Rose nodded. "See the wet one over there? She's had her eye on my guppies for weeks. And now I've caught her with her hand in the guppy jar, so to speak. Arrest her, Officer."

"I can explain everything," Sharon said. "I've been bugging them about playing this stupid old tape of me at this show, and I talked them into breaking in so we could watch it."

Claire frowned. "Jeez, Sharon, that's the best you can do? I'd have thought you'd be a much better liar."

"Ma'am, it's up to you if you want to press charges," the second policeman said.

"That won't be necessary," Rose said, rubbing her eyes wearily. "I'd much rather punish them myself. Especially guppy girl over there."

"May I please remove my hand now?" Jenna begged.

"I suppose. Don't make any sudden moves, though," Claire said. She and Rose walked the police to the door. They returned a moment later, wearing suspiciously wide grins.

"What are you two so happy about?" Jenna asked as she shook off her arm.

"We realized we've just found our permanent feed crew," Rose replied. She turned to leave. "And if this ever happens again, you won't be feeding the horses, girls. We'll be feeding you *to* the horses."

She flicked off the light and the girls followed them outside. The air was still and cold. Suddenly Claire let out a snort of laughter. "Okay," she said, pointing at the ground, "who owns the bunny slippers?"

"They're moose," Jenna said irritably.

"Sorry," Rose said, "but you girls just aren't cut out for a life of crime."

"Rose?" Jenna called as she and Claire walked away. "Don't tell Daniel about this, okay? It'll destroy her. She had such high hopes for our tent." Jenna turned to the others. "Sorry," she said. "I guess it wasn't exactly the perfect crime."

"It wasn't bad for our first time," Melissa said.

"Still, we are the Thoroughbrats," Katie pointed out. "We have a reputation to uphold."

"Oh, I think our reputation's intact," Sharon said. She nodded at the stable. "I'm going to take a little walk by the stable, but I'll be back to the tent soon."

"You want company?" Katie asked.

"No, thanks. I'll be fine, really." Sharon started to leave, then paused. "You know what?" she said. "I think we may have just bonded. Daniel's going to be so proud."

Sharon headed over to the nearest training ring. The white fence glowed faintly in the pale starlight. She leaned against it. There was no way she could sleep, not right now. She was sad, sadder than she had been in ages, but it was a different kind of sadness. She felt empty, lighter than air. If she let go of the fence, she might well have floated away like a balloon.

In the stable, someone whinnied softly. Luna. Sharon knew her tone already. Defiant. A tone that said *keep your distance, human. I won't get burned twice.*

A sentiment Sharon understood.

She unlatched the stable door and shoved it to the side. Luna was awake in her stall. Her eyes glowed.

"I don't know why I'm here," Sharon whispered. "It's not like we're making any progress, you and I."

Luna blinked. She approached Sharon doubtfully.

"I should go to bed," Sharon said.

Luna nudged her hand, then backed up two steps. Sharon smiled. "Or not."

She went to the tack room and returned a moment later with the lunge line, whip, and cavesson. She put the halter on Luna and led her out into the dark, damp air. Luna's gray coat caught hold of the scant starlight.

Luna was oddly calm. Strange. Maybe she was just sleepy. Maybe the night was calming her. It simplified everything, removed all the daytime distractions.

Sharon led her to the center of the ring. She felt less distracted, too. There was no one to see her fail. No one to see her tire, or look away in embarrassment if she tripped. It was just her and Luna, listening to the night music of crickets and leaves.

Sharon shortened the lunge line and positioned her whip. "Walk," she said firmly, tugging and tapping simultaneously.

Of course, nothing happened.

She tried again. Luna sniffed the air, then tossed her head toward the heavens.

"Walk," Sharon said, and this time it was more of a plea than a command.

All at once, even before Sharon could tug the line, Luna began to walk. It was an easy, graceful, I-trust-you walk. She flowed along like her limbs were water, carving a circle in the starlit ring.

She didn't balk. She didn't tense. She wasn't fighting Sharon anymore. Or maybe Sharon wasn't fighting her.

This isn't so bad, Luna seemed to be saying with her ears and her eyes and her relaxed body. *So this is what you wanted. Why didn't you just say so?*

It was working. Sharon didn't know why, but it was.

After a while she brought Luna to a gentle halt. She walked over and praised her, stroking and carrying on. Then she went over to the fence to rest her aching legs for a while.

So. She had finally gotten through to Luna. What had made her come back out tonight to try again? In the old days she never would have had the patience to put up with a horse like Luna. Even with Cass, she was always pushing, always trying to move to that next step just a little too fast.

Sharon thought of Randall. Randall, who could weave and fake and dribble with the best of them. Of Courtney, who could dance every dance in her wheelchair Mercedes.

She thought of Allegra, who always gave people the benefit of the doubt.

A black shape moved in the air. An owl? A hawk, maybe? It swooped past, then let itself be swallowed up in a leafy cave of dark trees.

Tears came again, surprising her. Tears for Cass, for that perfect flight she'd never take again.

She looked at Luna. Moonlight spilled from the filly's eyes. "Come," Sharon said, her voice choked.

Luna looked at her. Sharon let the line go slack and drop to the ground. She waited. "Come," she said again.

Luna took a step, paused, then took another. She nickered softly, to make it clear this was really *her* idea.

And then she walked the rest of the way to Sharon.

Sharon wrapped her arms around Luna's neck and hugged her close so that Luna would know she'd made the right choice. "Way to go, Luna-tic," she whispered.

It wasn't exactly a perfect flight over a triple bar, but it was enough.

Maybe Melissa was right. Maybe there were lots of ways to fly.

Sharon heard steps and turned. Katie and Melissa and Jenna were coming to get her.

She thought of Cassidy again, of her dream.

There's something I have to tell you, Cass, Sharon whispered. *It'll be okay. It's going to be okay.*

And this time she knew it was true.